Collecting Zebras
Stories From Hartford

Amanda Hamm

ISBN: 978-0-9850659-7-3

Collecting Zebras is a work of fiction. All names, characters, places, events, etc are products of the author's imagination or are used fictitiously.

Chapter 1

The poor guy was sitting in front of me at church. He was very handsome and appeared close to my age. Since we were at the same church, we clearly had tons in common and would get along well. I was thinking about how many months we would need to date before we could start planning a wedding when I noticed that he was sitting next to a woman. There was something similar in their jaw lines – at least from the back – that let me dismiss her as his sister. The sparkling diamond on her left hand did not escape my notice, but I knew she had to be engaged to someone else. Then everyone began to turn to their neighbors to shake hands and the guy in front of me turned to the woman next to him and gave her a quick – though not familial – kiss.

That's when I let my imagination begin forming a wild story about how this good-looking guy who was so obviously perfect for me might discover a family connection to his sweetheart. I was thinking something like second cousins once removed. That would be distant enough that I didn't have to imagine any estrangements for him to not know about the connection earlier. But it would be close enough that they would start to feel weird about getting married. Maybe. I threw cold water on the fantasy before I could work out all the details. I had already spent months feeling glad that no one could read my thoughts and now I could add this ludicrous story to the list.

I stayed in the pew when everyone else left as penance for being distracted. I found myself staring up at the large crucifix. Whoever carved it must have been very skilled. He or she had made Jesus into a fairly nice-looking…

I folded my arms across the back of the pew in front of me so I could drop my head and not crack it on the wood. What was wrong with me? Why was every male suddenly subject to scrutiny by my hormones? I wasn't a silly teenager. I was a 28-year-old

1

professional. And yet my newly man-crazed mind kept reaching new lows. I left through the side door of the church. There was a small chance that St. Christopher's new priest was still greeting people. He was fairly young and I needed to save the energy of policing my thoughts for later in the day.

It was moving day. I tried to cheer myself up with that thought because I had been looking forward to this moving day almost since my last one. But my brother-in-law had recruited two completely unknown (to me) guys to help. I sincerely hoped neither of them had showered in the last month because I was pretty sure that was the only way I would get through the afternoon without embarrassing myself.

****

Ashley had just gotten out of bed when I got back to the house. She was sitting at the kitchen table poking a spoon around a half-eaten bowl of cereal. She was still in her pajamas and her hair was pulled into a messy brown ponytail on top of her head.

"Are you eating today?" I asked.

"I'm trying. Honestly, I don't feel sick. I just have zero appetite."

I shrugged. "I really don't know when the whole 'eating for two' thing is supposed to kick in."

Ashley looked down and said, "Why aren't you hungry?"

I wasn't sure if she was talking to her stomach or the tiny person growing inside it. I didn't want to blame that tiny person for anything, but it was partly his or her fault. Ashley was my *younger* sister. It was bad enough when she beat me to the altar and now she was having a baby. It wasn't a race and it wasn't any other type of competition. I knew that. I also knew that Ashley was winning.

"Hey, Angel, how was church?" Jeff asked as he appeared in the doorway. He was obviously fresh from a shower, wearing gray shorts and a sweatshirt. He looked ready to help me move out. Though he was a perfectly nice guy, Jeff was the reason I was eager to get my own place. I had lived with Ashley for a while after school so moving in with her temporarily hadn't seemed like a big deal at the time. But there is a huge difference between living with your sister and living with your sister *and her husband.*

2

"Church was fine," I said.

"Which priest did you get?"

"Father Will."

"Awesome." Jeff pumped his fist slightly. "That means we'll probably have Father John tonight."

I tried not to roll my eyes. Jeff liked Father John because he frequently forgot to turn off his microphone and began most homilies by reminding the congregation that they were welcome to throw hymnals at him if he talked too long. He was eighty-two years old and had likely been making that same joke for more than fifty years. Jeff was not the only one who still laughed.

"I got you a bowl, too," Ashley said to her husband. She gestured to an empty bowl and spoon at the place next to hers.

"Thanks, honey," Jeff said as he sat and grabbed the box of cereal. "But you're supposed to let me wait on you."

I knew it must have been very strenuous for Ashley to take down a second bowl, but I kept the snarky comment to myself. "Your friends are coming at 11?"

Jeff swallowed quickly as he nodded. "They might be a bit earlier."

"You work with Luke but not Jon, right?"

"Yeah."

"So how do you know Jon?"

"I don't. Luke recruited him."

"Hmm…" I was going to begin my life in Hartford indebted to a complete stranger and my brother-in-law's boss. I tried not to think that wouldn't be so bad if one of them turned out to be attractive and available. I tried harder not to think that I might settle for available. "I guess I better change," I said as I left the cute couple alone.

Jeff and Ashley were cute because they matched. They were both tall and skinny, though Jeff was taller and Ashley was skinnier. They both had light brown hair, light blue eyes and slightly tipped up noses. They were also cute because they seemed so happy together. It was difficult for an extremely single older sister not to want to gag at the sight of them.

I went into my bedroom and closed the door. Jeans and a light purple top were waiting on my bed. The bed and the casual outfit were nearly the only things not already boxed. I slipped out of my church dress and into the waiting outfit. The dress I folded and put into the least full box of clothes. The sheets and comforter from my bed I wadded up and stuffed into garbage bags. No one was going to be seeing my bedding any time soon. Why should I care if it was a wrinkled mess?

There was a bathroom just outside my room and I stopped in front of the mirror before heading downstairs. The outfit was comfortable yet flattering. I gathered my long brown hair into a high ponytail and loosened a few sections to give it a messy-on-purpose look, which was much different from Ashley's bed head hair.

Ashley might have thought the same thing because she put her hand to her head as I reached the bottom of the stairs. She said, "I think I'm going to hide in our room when the guys get here."

Jeff had just stood up to clear their late breakfast from the table. He bent and kissed the top of Ashley's head. "Go ahead and rest as much as you need."

I didn't blame Ashley for wanting to stay out of the way. I tried to focus on that more generous thought instead of the irrational annoyance I felt at Jeff treating her like some sort of invalid. I had guessed they were expecting before they told me. He dropped the dishes in the sink as the doorbell rang and Ashley nimbly sprinted up the stairs.

"Hey, Luke," Jeff said as he opened the front door. "Thanks for coming to help out."

"You're welcome." I came close enough to get a peek at the newcomer as he came through the door and gestured behind himself. "Um, Jon got a phone call as we pulled up so he'll be just a minute."

Jeff nodded and closed the door before he turned to me. "This is my sister-in-law, Angel. It's her stuff we'll be dropping today."

"Very funny," I said. I smiled anyway as Luke glanced my way. He had the most amazing eyes I had ever seen. They were a wonderful deep blue, like a pristine lake at sunset. I could definitely take a swim in those eyes. And no wedding ring. And I knew he was employed.

And he immediately turned to Jeff and said, "I noticed you checked in code after midnight three times this week. I thought you were going to stop doing that."

Luke was apparently not interested in me. Or he was simply more subtle than I was. I stepped back to let the guys talk shop and

4

kind of wanted to smack myself in the head for trying to flirt with the guy who was only here to carry my heavy boxes. A light knock on the door said the phone conversation was over. I stayed just past the entryway as Jeff opened the door again. The guy on the other side was nearly as tall as Jeff, but with broader shoulders and darker hair. He said, "Sorry about the delay."

"No problem," Luke said. "Jon, this is Jeff and that's Angel. She doesn't want us to drop her things."

Jon looked a bit uncertain, but he sensed there was a joke and smiled as he said, "I'll do my best." He was even more attractive when he smiled. It made me feel warm all over. And there was definitely some sort of pheromone thing happening. And his ring finger was bare, too. And I didn't even know his last name. My one-track mind needed to find a new tune, at least for a little while.

A voice in my head was screaming at me to stop it… stop studying the volunteers and focus on showing them my bed. Great, now the voice was making me blush and all three of the guys were looking at me. I turned to lead them up the stairs to the things that needed moving. I pointed to the bed as we entered the room Jeff and Ashley let me use for free. "The bed needs to fit in the truck. It's the only thing I can't fit in my car if we don't get it all today."

Luke nodded.

Jon said, "Okay, we'll start with the bed then." He and Jeff each grabbed a side of the mattress and I volunteered to run ahead and get the door. That was a good "girl" job, helpful yet not strenuous. I stepped outside to hold the door as soon as I heard them coming. The weather could not have been more perfect for moving. It was sunny, but only about 65 degrees. I could probably carry some boxes without getting all sweaty and gross. That was important because I was hoping to make a good impression on Jon. And maybe Luke. I hadn't ruled him out, but I was feeling particularly attracted to Jon, the man I had known for approximately one minute. It took me only one minute to hope to get a date out of moving day. I was approximately pathetic.

Jon backed through the door first. He glanced at me only long enough to nod his gratitude at my extraordinary door holding. The porch was very small though and he appeared to be concentrating on not falling down the steps behind him. That left me free to check him out more thoroughly.

He was carrying the mattress as though it hardly weighed anything so he was clearly strong. His dark hair was slightly long. It looked as though he wore it that way on purpose as opposed to needing a haircut reminder. I liked it, but it made him look rather young. Or maybe he *was* that young. I had to remind myself again that I knew almost nothing about this guy I was practically drooling over. He reached the sidewalk and looked up at me through his lashes.

I attempted a natural smile to cover for the fact that I had been caught staring at him. I think he was going to return the smile. That's when he dropped his end of the mattress.

Jeff banged against the door I was holding as he struggled to keep his balance. The mattress wobbled against the railing before Jon could hoist his end again. I was feeling better about my prospects. As soon as he had a good grip though, he said, "Sorry about that. The handle broke."

"That's okay," Jeff said. "We got the dropping out of the way now."

The two guys continued towards the red pickup in the driveway while I mashed my ego back into place. Jon hadn't dropped the mattress because I made him nervous, but because I bought a mattress with lousy handles. One of them had separated from the fabric when we carried it into the house as well. In hindsight, it might have been a good idea to warn someone about that.

When I got back upstairs, Luke had tipped the box springs against the wall and was working to dismantle the frame. I positioned myself on the opposite end and began to loosen the wing nuts. I tried to catch Luke's eye, tried to detect whether or not he might be looking for an opportunity to check me out. I tried to give him an excuse and said, "I guess I expected Jeff's boss to be older."

"I guess I got an early start," Luke replied, without looking up at all. Then he said, "I didn't go upstairs much."

"What?"

"Oh, I..." Luke looked in my general direction. "Sorry, this carpet just reminded me of something."

I wanted to ask what it reminded him of because I wanted to keep those eyes facing me but Jon and Jeff returned and they each grabbed an end of the waiting box springs.

Jon said, "I'll see if I can make Jeff drop this one." His smile was nearly imperceptible but the comment was clearly for my enjoyment. I couldn't figure out if I should focus my attention on Luke or Jon next, but my attention should have been on the bed frame. The wing nut I was absently twisting back and forth fell off the end of the screw and the side of the frame fell against my leg. The only part that hurt was that I had to come back to reality.

I ran down the stairs ahead of the next part of my bed, telling myself on each step that I was moving out of my sister's house… not shopping for a man. I found a way to prop the door and went back upstairs to pick up a box.

It didn't take very long for four people to empty the room. I managed to stay focused the rest of the time, saying to the guys only things directly related to our task such as… "That one's heavy," "That one might be fragile," and "No, a person cannot have too many zebras." None of these comments could be construed as attempts to flirt.

The four of us somehow ended up gathered in the empty bedroom. Luke seemed to be examining the impressions my bed had left in the carpet. Jon was looking expectantly at Jeff so I also turned to Jeff. "I guess we got it all," I said.

"Yeah… so I was thinking we could hit the drive-through down the street and then eat lunch on the way to Hartford."

"Didn't you finish breakfast like five minutes before these guys showed up?"

Jeff shrugged. "I could still eat."

I had learned that he was very efficient. It would probably bother him to have a 30-minute drive consist of nothing but driving. And I was a bit hungry myself. "Okay," I said, "I guess that'll be better than stopping in the middle of unloading and I know there's no food at my place yet anyway."

The other guys nodded and we went out the front door. Jeff moved the big rock to let it close. "Hey, Jon," he said, "do you mind riding with Angel so I can pick Luke's brain about a work thing?"

Luke said something about not wanting to spend too much time on work on a Sunday. I don't know Jon's initial reaction to the suggestion because *my* reaction was to rush to move the suitcase out of the front seat of my car. It hadn't occurred to me that I might have a passenger.

7

"Do you have room for me?" Jon asked as he arrived at the side of my car.

"Of course." I shut the back door on my small silver car. "It's not that full. I was just trying to keep track of my suitcase."

He nodded and opened the passenger door. I tried not to skip on my way around the car. I hope no one could tell that I was skipping on the inside. A guy I found physically appealing was going to be stuck in the car with me for the next half hour. That should give me time to work out a few more details about him. If he was unavailable though, it would be best for me to learn that in the early part of the drive. Otherwise, I was going to be mentally picking out a bridesmaid dress for Ashley before we got to Hartford.

I admit it. I had already noted that she looked fabulous in pink.

Chapter 2

I slid behind the wheel of my car and inhaled a wonderfully unfamiliar scent. Thank you, pleasant weather. I was not the only one who could move a few boxes and stay fresh. I waited for the red truck with my bed in the back to pull out of the driveway and then I began to follow it. Jon hadn't said a word since I got into the car and I couldn't think of anything before Awkward Silence invaded the scene. That was bad. Now I had to think extra carefully about what to say. If I threw out a topic and it fell flat, Awkward Silence would become Uncomfortably Awkward Silence.

I tried to appear thoughtful rather than anxious. Perhaps there was a chance I could pretend that I was only quiet because I was trying to make sure I hadn't forgotten anything. Fortunately, the drive-through Jeff had mentioned was very close. As I turned in, I asked Jon what he wanted to eat. He gave me an order and then made a move to pay for it.

"No way," I said. "You don't even know me and you're helping me move. The very least I can do is buy you a sandwich."

Jon put his wallet back in his pocket. "I don't think I can insist when you put it like that."

"It wouldn't have done you any good to insist. So, um, how long have you and Luke been friends anyway?"

"We're not really. I mean, I don't know him that well. He just recently started dating one of my sister's friends."

Interesting. Luke was dating someone. Jon had a sister. I grabbed the two drinks and slipped them into the cup holders before I took the bag of food from the person at the window and passed it to Jon. He took out his sandwich and fries and passed the bag back to me. I only ordered fries because that seemed like the easiest thing to eat while driving. Jon said nothing about it and that was a point in his favor. I once dated a guy who always commented on what I was eating. By the end of the fairly short relationship, I'd

9

wanted to serve him up a big bowl of I'll-eat-whatever-I-want-thank-you-very-much.

"If you don't really know Luke or Jeff, how did you get roped into helping out today?"

"I don't remember whose idea it was but… well, I wasn't doing anything else today." He shrugged as though helping out a total stranger was no big deal.

I liked carnations, white ones. They were humble flowers that would look lovely with pink ribbon that matched Ashley's dress.

Jon said, "How careful do I have to be with this food in your car?"

"I can deal with anything that happens accidentally."

"Okay. That seems about right. It looks like a happy medium in here."

"What does that mean?"

"I see a lot of cars – I'm a mechanic – and I've seen some pigsties and at least one car where I felt like I should take off my shoes before stepping on the floor mats."

A mechanic. It might be handy to know a mechanic even if he was never going to propose to me. I stuffed a few fries into my mouth and told myself to shut up even though I hadn't said that out loud.

"Can I ask you something?" Jon asked.

I nodded.

"Jeff is your brother-in-law because he's married to your sister, right?"

"Yes?" His tone sounded as though the first question was the lead-in to the real question.

"Where was your sister today?"

"Oh, she was at the house. She was hiding."

Jon smiled slightly. "Hiding?"

"She felt weird about being there and not helping. But she has a good excuse. She's pregnant."

"How, um… when is she due?"

"Not for another six months. She doesn't look pregnant yet and that's why she thought it would look like she should be helping."

"Oh. Can I ask you something else?"

"The drive to Hartford is going to seem a lot longer if we sit here not talking."

10

"I was just going to ask why you were staying with your sister. That feels like a story, but if it's too personal you don't have to share."

I shook my head. "I don't mind. It's kind of a long story though so you might be sorry you asked." I glanced to his side of the car to see if he still wanted to ask a question if it had a long answer. He bumped his eyebrows up with interest and I turned the AC knob up a notch while I mentally gave him another point for being cute. "Okay," I said. "I guess it starts with Ashley – that's my sister's name – and Jeff. They met online and dated sort of semi-long-distance for a little over a year before they decided to get married. Ashley and I were sharing an apartment in, um, actually... I'm not going to tell you where we were living because I don't have anything good to say about that place at the moment. But let's just say it's almost a hundred and fifty miles from here.

"Jeff and Ashley got together in person about every other Saturday and otherwise did a lot of emailing and FaceTime. So Ashley moved to Port Harris when they got married and she almost immediately started begging me to follow her. She's less than two years younger than me and has always been my best friend. But she also knew I was fairly miserable where I was.

"It was my first job out of grad school. Um, I'm a speech therapist. I did some interning while I was at school, which was great, and I thought I'd find a job like that where I could help little kids. But where I worked, it was a pretty affluent part of town and most of the kids... they didn't need help. The kids were cute and all, but they all had these pretentious parents who were trying to use therapy to give their kids some sort of academic edge. You know, wanting to be able to brag about how many words their toddlers could say. And my boss was a horrible person.

"I hate to say that because it makes me sound like her. She was horrible because she always had something negative to say about everyone else. She was the sort of person who would compliment a woman's shoes to her face and then turn around and tell me she couldn't believe anyone would buy such ugly shoes and that they made the wearer look fat. I mean really, how do shoes make a person look fat? It was as though she invented ways to insult people."

I heard Jon chuckle, which meant he wasn't bored yet so I kept talking. "My commute was bad, too. And yes, that was sort of my

11

own fault. I found an apartment that I thought would be twenty minutes from work, but I failed to test it during rush hour. I had to drive around forty-five minutes each way so it felt like I was spending all my time either at work or driving to or from work.

"So with Ashley bugging me, I did start putting my resume out to some places in Port Harris. And I got a nibble. I got an interview at a private practice fairly close to where Jeff and Ashley live. I thought it went *very* well. At that time, I had two weeks to either renew my lease or move out of my apartment. I thought God had everything timed out perfectly for me. Two weeks to move out meant I could give two weeks' notice at my old job and I figured Ashley could help me pick a place in Port Harris. And she did actually. It was a great place. But I didn't get the job."

Jon said, "Uh, oh."

"Yeah... I found that out the day *after* I quit the old one."

"I can't believe they didn't hire you."

"Thank you. But anyway, since I had to look for a new job no matter what, I figured I might as well do it in Port Harris. Jeff and Ashley insisted I move in with them to save money and to make sure I got an apartment that was convenient to wherever I ended up working. I've been with them since the first of August and it's okay except that... well, Jeff works from home and Ashley doesn't have a job so they're both *always* there. And Ashley is *always* talking about the baby."

Jon nodded understandingly. "I can see how that could be rough. I have kind of a big family and I love them all but... there are limits."

"Exactly. I guess the end of the story then is that I found a job in Hartford at the end of August and while I found a great house to rent right away, it wasn't available until October. So here we are."

"I went to Hartford Elementary. The offices where you work were added more recently though."

"Yeah, I can tell that part is newer. The offices are very nice and... wait a minute. How do you know where I work?"

Jon laughed as though I had asked a stupid question. He said, "Hartford is very small so new people tend to get noticed. You should assume at least half the town knows where you work."

"Really?"

"Oh, yeah. If you ever want to know what people know about you – or at least what they're saying – all you have to do is talk to my aunt Mabel."

I ate a few handfuls of fries while I thought about this. I wasn't sure how I felt about living somewhere I might be exceptionally noticed. I wondered how long that would take to wear off.

Apart from an occasional house or barn, there wasn't much in the way of scenery in the gap between Port Harris and Hartford. And a majority of the drive was in this gap. The most interesting thing to look at was in the front yard of a house we were about to pass. It was some sort of animal roughly carved out of a large old tree trunk. I think it might have been about four feet high and the bottom half was a bark-covered base.

I pointed it out to Jon. "I think that weird animal sculpture might be the most interesting thing on this drive."

"It's a bear," he said. "It's more interesting now than it used to be."

"How did it get more interesting?"

"There was a, um… I'm going to say scandal but I'm using the word loosely, around the bear a few years ago."

"A wooden bear scandal? You're going to have to tell me that story."

"All right." Jon had finished his burger. He crumpled up the wrapper and tried to put on a serious expression. He still looked amused as he said, "It was stolen. Sort of. It disappeared and the guy who carved it reported it stolen. It was all anyone in town could talk about for a few days and it was funny because you knew everyone was thinking, 'Who would take an ugly bear statue?' but they were trying to be nicer than to come out and say that. Then the bear was returned and people couldn't help themselves. Jokes were flying about how maybe it had been a blind thief who returned it when his friends explained what he'd taken or that someone had been paid to take it and then paid even more to give it back."

"That's terrible." I felt sort of bad for the guy, but I admit I was laughing, too.

"So it turned out that his kids – I think they were like thirteen and fourteen at the time – had gotten together a few friends to cart it off as a prank. They were going to put it back the next day but once the police were involved they were too afraid of getting in trouble. Eventually they confessed to their dad and I guess he was

13

embarrassed about calling the police on his kids so he helped them bring it back in the middle of the night. But there were enough people involved that it didn't take long for the real story to come out. The gossip faded pretty quickly once people knew what happened."

I enjoyed the story and I especially enjoyed listening to Jon tell it, but it didn't get me any closer to finding out if he was available. I needed to be cautious about how much I was enjoying his company. I needed to switch to a topic that might lead to talking about me or him or the possibility of a me *and* him. I tried, "When you signed up to help today, did they tell you there would be more work on the Hartford end? Most of my furniture was put in storage when I moved to Port Harris. It should have been delivered yesterday so there *should* be a container of heavy-lifting waiting for us."

"Yes, I was warned about having to move stuff while helping someone move. And yes, your container was delivered."

I glanced at Jon. He didn't seem to think there was anything weird about what he had just said. "You know where I live, too?" I asked. He didn't say anything and when I glanced back, he was grinning at my disbelief. It wasn't fair. He was ridiculously cute even when he was being smug.

"All right," he said after a moment. "I'll connect the dots for you. Caitlin Anshire is my sister."

"Oh!" I knew Caitlin. She worked in the office at the school and we'd become friendly. I tried to think of anything she might have said about a brother. The only thing I could remember for sure was that she'd said she had three of them. Anything else may or may not have applied to Jon. I felt significantly disadvantaged. Though I was sure I had told Caitlin why I was living with my sister and that information hadn't been passed on.

"Are you worried about what else she might have told me?" Jon's attitude was teasing. Was he flirting with me!? Maybe there was a chance my fantasies weren't being wasted on this guy.

Chapter 3

I was excited about my new house in Hartford. Even though I was still renting, a house felt more grownup than an apartment. It was one tiny step closer to the white picket fence dream. And it was a very cute house. It had fresh yellow siding and white shutters with hearts carved into them. It was a single story with two tiny bedrooms and one tiny bathroom. The kitchen and dining room could be separated by doors that slid right into the walls. Honesty, I couldn't imagine a time I'd want to separate those rooms, but the fact that I could was still very cool.

Jon and I had finished the drive pleasantly. That's a good word for it. He mentioned that his sister once pointed me out at church. That meant we went to the same one. I didn't like to think about it because it limited my options, but a shared faith was important to me. His off-hand comment was a welcome revelation. He told me a story about his dad that made me laugh so hard I almost choked on my drink. And there were a few more times I thought he might have been flirting. He never asked if I was seeing anyone though. Never asked for my phone number or otherwise said anything that showed clear interest. Maybe he was a little shy or maybe he was simply taking things more slowly. Maybe he would be the sane one in our relationship, the one who wasn't wondering whether we'd have a boy first or a girl before we had a single date.

I unlocked the storage container as soon as we arrived and was happy to see that the things inside looked familiar. I tried to carry as many boxes as I could, but kept getting interrupted by one or more guys asking me to which room something should be delivered. I felt more like a supervisor than a helper.

I did manage to work it so that I carried parts for the bed frame right behind Jon and Luke carrying the mattress. Then I asked Jon if he'd help me put the frame back together. I tried to make some meaningful eye contact, something that said he should make a move. I thought he might have understood, but then Jeff walked in and asked me where I wanted a box that appeared unlabeled.

I walked over and opened one of the flaps. "Its pans," I said, with a little too much impatience directed at someone who was doing me a favor.

He looked a bit sheepish. "Kitchen, huh?"

I nodded. He handed the box to me before I could turn back around. "It's not heavy. Why don't you take this and I'll help Jon with the bed?"

I took the box because that was the rational thing to do. We had finished the frame and the springs and mattress would be more work for Jon if I was the one helping him. I set the box on my kitchen counter and went outside to find something I could carry to the bedroom. There was a man walking a medium-sized dog on the sidewalk in front of my new house. He called out to me, "Hello. Are you the one moving in?"

"Yes, I am," I said as I walked up to him. "Angel Melling."

"Angel? What a pretty name. I'm George Baumgartner. I live right there." He pointed to a house across the street and to the right. "Are you moving in alone?" he asked with a glance towards Luke, who was exiting the container with a large box.

"Yeah, it's just me." His question seemed casual. A part of my brain processed the fact that he *might* be asking if I was single. I quickly began to assess whether or not that *might* be a promising development. The touch of gray in his otherwise dark hair said that he was probably older than me. The lines around his eyes were faint though. And he had no ring on his left hand. And he seemed friendly. And his dog was just about the cutest thing I had ever seen. "What's his name?" I asked with a nod in that direction.

"Mutt."

I didn't mean to look offended on the dog's behalf, but I must have showed some sort of reaction to the name because George looked apologetic.

"That's the name they gave him at the shelter," he said. "And he responded to it so I felt like I shouldn't change it."

"He's absolutely adorable. Can I pet him?"

"Sure. Mutt, sit."

The dog promptly put his rear on the sidewalk and kept it there even though his tail was swinging wildly from side to side as I knelt to stroke his ears. He had short brown fur with black and gray speckles along his back. His ears were floppy and his muzzle short. He slipped his pink tongue onto my wrist a few times while I scratched behind his amazingly soft ear. His eyes darted between me and George as though making sure he was doing a good job greeting me and I immediately fell in love with Mutt. Even his name was suddenly cute. "How long have you had him?" I asked.

"More than ten years. He was probably around two when I got him."

"He's so well behaved. Does he do tricks?"

"Yeah, he likes to show off."

I stood up to give them some room and George said, "Up!" Mutt jumped to his hind legs.

"Mutt, dance." George moved his hand in a circle and Mutt hopped around to follow it. "Good boy." George gave the dog some firm pats as Mutt returned to all four legs looking very pleased with himself. George turned back to me. "He knows more, but we need to save some for next time we run into you, right?"

I nodded. "I'm already impressed though. So, um, how long have you lived over there?" I pointed at the same house he had indicated earlier.

"Longer than I've had Mutt. It's a nice street."

"Anything a newcomer should know?"

George looked thoughtful for a moment. "Not particularly. It's pretty quiet here. Oh, there's one thing though. There's an older couple down the street that way..." He tipped his head to my right. I looked in that direction. "It's the darker blue house," he said. "They sit out on the porch a lot and invite passersby to join them. They're very nice, but you should only accept if you have lots of time to kill."

"Talkers, huh?"

"Oh, yeah. I've sat with them a few times and like I said... They're very nice, but it's hard to get away."

"Hey, Angel, where does this go?"

I turned and saw Jon holding a lamp, the base of which was shaped like a very fat zebra. "Um, living room." He nodded and took it into the house.

"Got a Thorpe helping you? You're in Hartford now," George said. He seemed to be referring to Jon, but I didn't know his last name.

"Is that his name?" I asked. "One of these guys is married to my sister and I don't actually know the other two."

"Any time you don't know someone's last name in Hartford, Thorpe is a fairly good guess. There are about a million of them."

"Actually, I think I have met at least one Thorpe already."

George nodded. "See?"

"Well, it was great to meet you, but I really shouldn't let these guys keep doing all the work."

"Yeah, I'll get out of your way. Come on, Mutt." George led Mutt past my house and I grabbed a light box from the trunk of my car.

Even with the waiting furniture, I didn't own a ton of stuff. When the container seemed close to empty, I began to look around for the most important things to unpack. I started in the kitchen and had only unpacked one box when Jon wandered in.

"Anything I can do in here?" he asked.

It may have been wishful thinking, but I got the impression he was looking for an excuse to be near me. "Well..." I looked around, eager to give him a reason to stay. "That one is pans. I think I'm going to keep those in that cupboard." I pointed and he opened the box. "Is your last name Thorpe?" I asked.

He seemed confused when he looked at me. "It is. Didn't I tell you that?"

I shook my head.

"Oh, sorry." He offered his hand to me. "Jonathon Thorpe."

"Angel Melling. But I think you knew that." He smiled when I took his hand and I tried to pretend I didn't feel electricity from head to toe at the feel of his rough, strong grip. I think he felt something as well though because he let go quickly and looked nervous as he reached into the box of pans.

"So, um..." he started.

I held my breath, sure he was about to ask if I might be free to get together sometime.

Jon pulled out a pan and said, "Who told you my last name?"

"Oh, I just met one of my neighbors. He said if I didn't know someone's last name I should guess Thorpe because there are a million of them in Hartford."

"A slight exaggeration, but there are a lot of us. My dad's mom and dad had eleven kids and nine of them were boys so they kept the name and every one of them has at least two kids, a lot of whom also have kids."

"I know there's a kindergarten teacher named Thorpe. Her first name is…"

Jon nodded before I could remember it. "She's my cousin," he said.

I was sure I had met someone else with the name. I couldn't recall where I had heard it though so I reached into the box in front of me and began to unwrap a ceramic zebra-shaped cookie jar.

"What is with all the zebras anyway?"

I shrugged. "Most of them have been gifts. Sometime in high school I decided I liked zebras. Word got out and people started giving them to me. I guess that makes me easy to shop for except… Well, there are a few that I don't display."

Jon laughed. Jeff came in and said, "I'm telling Ashley you said her zebra was ugly."

I pointed to the cookie jar. "Ashley's zebra gets a place of honor."

"I'm still telling," he teased.

Luke walked in behind Jeff and the kitchen started to feel rather small. "Everything's in the house now," he said. "How much help do you want unpacking?"

"You can go," I said. "I was planning to do most of it later and I need to buy some food and…"

"You want us to get out of your way now," Jeff finished for me.

"I really do appreciate all the help."

Luke said, "You're welcome," and then turned to Jon. "You want a ride?"

"Sure." Jon waved to me. "I'll probably see you again soon, small town and all."

"Right. Thanks again, both of you."

Jeff also thanked the two extra guys and walked them out. Then he returned to the kitchen and said, "Are you ready to drive back to Port Harris now?"

"Why?"

He stared at me until it sank in.

"Oh," I said. "Why didn't you bring your car?"

"That was your sister's brilliant idea."

I sighed and picked up my purse and car keys. The sooner I started the extra hour of driving, the sooner I could yell at Ashley about it. "What was she trying to accomplish by having me give you a ride?"

Jeff rolled his eyes. "She was trying to play match-maker."

"What?"

"She told me that if either of the guys was single that I should try to have him ride with you. I didn't know about Jon so…" Jeff shrugged and started out the door.

"How did she talk you into going along with that?"

"You don't want to know."

"I'm going to take your word for that." I might have to hold off on yelling at Ashley. The drive with Jon had been good and if he ended up asking me out, I'd have to admit she had an excellent idea.

Chapter 4

Monday morning it took me more time to find the shoes I wanted to wear than it took me to drive to work. Small town life had its perks.

I got to the school early because of the short drive and wandered over to the fourth and fifth grade hallway. Parker Jones taught fourth grade and I considered him my most serious prospect in the building. As far as I had learned, he was the only man there who was both single and under fifty. Yes, I was desperate enough that single and under fifty were the only criteria I needed to declare someone a serious prospect. It wasn't as though I was going to propose to him, I was only trying to make myself show up on his radar.

I poked my head through his doorway. "Good morning, Parker. Ready for Monday?"

He groaned playfully as he looked up. "Maybe we should only have Mondays every other week."

"Yeah, that would work."

"Hey, you could at least *try* to like my idea."

"Picked up on the sarcasm, huh?"

Parker pushed his chair away from his desk and let it swivel towards me. "Did you get all moved in this weekend?"

"Yes. I am already loving the 3-minute commute."

"Awesome. You're going to have extra time on your hands now."

"I know. Maybe I'll get a hobby."

"Or… you could do something with me."

"Maybe," I said with my best coy smile. I left before he could suggest anything specific. Just because I was desperate didn't mean I had to act like it.

What everyone at Hartford Elementary called the office was actually a set of offices. Through the main door was the main office. The secretary's desk sat in the middle. A door to the nurse's office was on the right and a hallway lined with smaller offices was on the left. My office was one of those smaller ones. Though I worked at the school, I was technically employed by the county. Roughly half the kids I saw were too young for kindergarten and they were as much a part of my problem as Ashley's pregnancy. I spent hours a day with adorable kids who belonged to other people.

The kids were not always cute and that's how I knew I was in trouble. Sometimes they stuck fingers in their noses or ate things they dropped on the floor or thought they were telling jokes simply by saying the word "poop" over and over. The kids occasionally did disgustingly unlovable things and yet I still knew I would love to have one... or more.

My office was crammed with stuff, but it was more organized than my house at the moment. There was a bookcase on either side of the door, each filled with books and games. My desk was by the opposite wall, facing out. And a short table sat in the middle of the room surrounded by short chairs. I would start the day with back-to-back first graders, then have a quick break before my first preschooler.

The little ones were brought in by their moms and that was torture. All of those women seemed my age. To a four-year-old, only other four-year-olds are the same age. To a 28-year-old like me, pretty much all women in their twenties or thirties felt like the same age. And these women I was seeing every day were all so far ahead of me on the whole marriage and family thing. I envied the way the kids would run up and hug their moms as they left me. It made my biological clock skip right over ticking to a full alarm.

My first three-year-old of the day was a slightly shy boy named Ethan. He had been afraid to talk to me at our first session until I pulled out a game he remembered from his previous therapist. It was fairly smooth sailing after that, but I didn't like to think that I could be replaced in his life just as easily by someone else with hopping frogs. I remembered as I prepared for him that his last name was Thorpe. That was the other place I'd heard the name. I considered how he might be related to Jon. His dad must be either a brother or a cousin. I only knew his mom though. Her name was Heather. I wasn't sure if I'd see her that day because she was expecting her second child any time... if she hadn't delivered already.

The first time I met Heather she had been talking to Caitlin. Caitlin was always chatting with the moms while they waited. I thought she must know everyone in town and now I kind of wondered if that was because she was related to half of them. I remembered that particular conversation because Heather had been complaining about her husband. She said that she wished she could get him to wear his ring more often. I asked why he didn't and she said that it wasn't that he didn't want to wear it, but that he was a mechanic and would take if off for work and forget to put it back on. I tried to be sympathetic. I wanted to tell her she was lucky to have a husband to complain about.

Heather and Ethan were waiting in the main office when I came out to look for them. They were never late. "Good morning," I said. "I keep expecting you to show up with a baby."

Heather shook her head. "Not yet. I'm actually scheduled to be induced tomorrow morning though."

"All right. So you'll have a little girl next time I see you. Isn't that exciting, Ethan?"

Ethan glanced at me and then turned back to the car he was pushing on the floor.

Heather said, "Yeah, so my husband will bring Ethan on Wednesday and... well, we'll see how I'm feeling but I'll probably be back next Monday."

"Okay. Come on, Ethan, let's get started." The little boy took my offered hand and I led him back to my office. We played our half hour of games and then I wished him and his mom luck with the new arrival. Caitlin was there when they left. I asked her if she wanted to join me for lunch.

"Sorry," she said, "Dan's stopping by today. Rain check for tomorrow?"

"Sure." Dan was her husband. Of course she'd rather have lunch with him. I ate alone in my office. I got some extra work done though. I could almost be happy about that.

****

I had been avoiding the Hartford Market while I was only working in Hartford. It was a completely unappealing building, weathered and dreary. It didn't look like a nice place to shop, but I needed food. I had picked up a few things in Port Harris after I

23

dropped Jeff off. I had been too tired for a real shopping trip though. I pulled into the lot at the Market on my way home from work.

The automatic swinging doors looked kind of dangerous. Once I got inside, however, the store looked like a perfectly acceptable supermarket. It was a little small. I didn't exactly have exotic tastes so I figured it'd have everything I needed. I found enough food for a week or so and then made my way up front to pay for it.

The woman at the register was plump and grandmotherly, somehow like I'd picture the witch from Hansel & Gretel while she was still disguised. "Hi, hon," she said.

"Hi."

"Did you find everything?"

"I think so."

"I'm Mabel Thorpe and I don't know you so you must be new in town."

"Yes, I am. It's nice to meet you. I'm Angel Melling."

"Oh, right. You're over at the elementary school."

"That's right."

"Oh, hon, they are so happy with you over there."

I nodded appreciatively. That was good to hear. This must be the Mabel that Jon said would know what people were saying about me. "I like it, too," I said. "The kids are great."

"You moved in all by yourself, didn't you?"

"I had help, but I'm living alone if that's what you mean."

"I hear you met George Baumgartner already though."

There was something suggestive in Mabel's tone that made me hesitant to confirm her statement. It felt as though she was waiting to gauge my exact level of interest in the man I'd just met. I didn't want to tell her I was working on the same thing. "I did meet him… and his dog."

"Oh, Mutt is the cutest thing ever, isn't he? But George needs a nice girl. That one had a *tragic* divorce."

"He's divorced?" This felt like gossip, but I couldn't help myself.

Mabel nodded and leaned a bit closer while she continued to move my groceries across the scanner. "He was married almost four years. One day he came home from work to find that she had packed up and left with no warning. They say she didn't even leave a note. He tracked her down to see if they could work things out.

24

She wouldn't talk to him. Completely broke his heart. It's been years though. Could be he's ready for someone new."

A box had tipped over on the conveyor and I pretended to need all my attention to straighten it because I didn't know what to say.

"If George doesn't float your boat though, I have a few available nephews and Bill's trying to get his younger son hitched."

A slight laugh escaped as I realized this woman might be the only person as eager as I was to have me paired off. "I, um… I think I'm just here for groceries right now."

"All right." Mabel smiled and scanned a few items in silence before she said, "Any night you don't feel like cooking, Pops is really good. And they deliver."

"The pizza place? I haven't been there yet."

"You're missing out, hon. Try the Hartford Special." She gave a wink with the suggestion.

"I might do that sometime." My groceries had all been bagged and even though Mabel didn't announce a total, I knew how to use the card reader. I waved as she handed me the receipt and as I walked away I heard her telling the next person that someone's surgery had gone well.

I opened my trunk in the parking lot and placed a bag inside. When I turned to grab another, Jon Thorpe was standing in front of me. He was wearing a short sleeve navy work shirt that said Hartford Garage in white lettering on the pocket. It was unbuttoned with a plain white shirt underneath. I had a vision of slipping my hands between those shirts to give him a hug, as though welcoming him home from work. I said only, "Hi." I hoped he couldn't tell what I was thinking.

"You look surprised," he said. "I told you we'd probably see each other again soon." He reached into my cart and lifted the rest of my bags into my trunk in one load.

"Thanks." I closed the trunk and tried to think of something to say to keep him there. "I, um, just met Mabel. You said she was your aunt, right?"

"Yeah. She didn't grill you too much, did she? Sometimes she gets a little personal." He looked uneasy at the thought.

"No, she seems nice. She was giving me some pointers on the town."

He nodded.

"She told me I was missing out because I haven't been to Pops yet. Would you second that recommendation?"

"Definitely. Pops is awesome."

"She said I should try the Hartford Special. What's on that?"

Jon grinned at me. "I think you should call Pops and ask them. They'd get a kick out of it."

"Why would that be funny?"

"Saying Hartford Special is like code for 'surprise me.' They'll usually put on three or four toppings and only charge you for one so it's a good deal if you're feeling adventurous."

"So I'd embarrass myself if I called and asked what was on it? I can't believe you suggested that."

Jon cocked his head to the side as though he doubted I was upset. "I was kidding. I'm sure they would have thought you were, too."

"Well, I'm not too picky so maybe I'll give the Hartford Special a try sometime."

A faint smile appeared on his face. He put his arm up and rubbed the back of his neck while he looked at the ground. Why wasn't he picking up on the obvious? I was a helpless newcomer who needed a local to take me to Pops and show me what I was missing. He said, "I better let you get your food home. I'll take the cart for you."

"Hope to bump into you again soon," I said to his back. He might not have heard me over the rattling of the shopping cart. I got into my car and watched Jon enter the store. He didn't look back. I was sure there was a spark between us, but maybe he was only being friendly and whatever I felt was merely coming from me.

Chapter 5

There was a surprise on my front porch when I got home. Flowers! It had been years since anyone sent me flowers. I arranged the yellow and red blooms – perfect for early fall – on my kitchen table where I could appreciate them. I hadn't looked at the card yet. I had a feeling the bouquet was a house-warming gift from my parents and I wanted to delay that disappointment with a lovely daydream about a secret admirer.

I imagined a man at the school who had somehow escaped my notice. He would send me flowers every day this week before introducing himself. We would, of course, make an adorable couple. The only problem with my daydream was that when I tried to picture what this mystery man looked like… Jon's face inserted itself into my thoughts.

I gave up trying to make him look like anyone else and unfolded the card. It said, "Welcome to the neighborhood. George and Mutt."

That was unexpected. And more fun than flowers from my parents. I called Ashley. "Guess what?"

"What?" she asked.

"I think Parker is on the verge of asking me out *and* I just got flowers from one of my new neighbors."

"Wow."

"I know. Maybe being a novelty in town won't be so bad."

"What about Jon? Did you ask his sister if he's seeing anyone?"

"No. It feels a little… sixth grade to pump his sister for info. But of course I'm still keeping my ears open in case she lets something interesting slip."

"Of course."

I told Ashley about seeing Jon at the Market and she said that she missed me already. I appreciated the sentiment even though we

27

both knew she was glad to have me out of the house so she could start picturing that room as a nursery.

My doorbell rang shortly after I ended the call. I answered to a familiar older man and a second man closer to my age who was not familiar. The older one was my landlord. He looked like he might be in his late sixties and had mentioned being recently retired so that seemed about right. His name was Bill Iverson.

"Hi, Bill."

"Good evening, Miss Melling. How are you?"

"Fine, thanks. But you have to call me Angel if you expect me to call you Bill."

"Fair enough, Angel, dear. This is my youngest son, Riley." Bill motioned to the man next to him. Riley held out his hand to me rather stiffly. He appeared slightly uncomfortable.

"Nice to meet you," I said as I took his hand.

"So we just wanted to stop by," Bill said, "to make sure you got moved in okay yesterday. Any problems?"

"No, not at all. I'm still getting organized but the house is great."

"Glad to hear it. I know you have my contact information, but I thought a second person would be good in case, God forbid, you have any sort of emergency. Riley's going to give you his card, too."

Bill prompted his son with a nod and Riley pulled a business card out of his pocket. "I'm sure I can't think of a reason Dad won't be able to help you," he said.

"She is new in town," Bill said. "Having the acquaintance of a younger man might be nice for general help." The balding half of the duo looked between me and his son approvingly and I realized that he was making this introduction for more personal than professional reasons. I immediately scrutinized Riley. He was on the heavier side but tall and well proportioned. He gave off more of a teddy bear vibe than a linebacker vibe. He had sandy hair and light though very thick lashes that floated up and down in a hint of shyness. No wedding ring and his dad, who I thought was very nice, felt there was a possibility between us. I could be open to that possibility.

I took the card and smiled tentatively as I noted the Hartford Bank logo on the upper corner. "I'll keep this in a safe place in case I think of something I need."

"Perfect," Bill said. "We'll leave you alone to finish settling. Have a good evening."

"Nice to meet you, Angel," Riley said as he followed his dad from my porch.

I closed the door and tucked the business card into a side pocket in my purse.

****

Tuesday was a fairly ordinary day, by which I mean there were no developments on my hunt for a husband. Wednesday presented me with a major setback.

The morning began fine. My first kid of the day was out sick so I had a little extra time to chat with Caitlin. She and her husband (to whom she had been married only about six months) were living in a very old house and she always had a story about their remodeling attempts. This time they had taken out some old shelving and discovered that it had been installed to cover a door in the wall.

I sent a little girl named Emily back to class and then stayed in my office to make a few notes. I had forgotten that Heather said her husband would bring Ethan until I walked down the short hallway and found a man sitting next to the familiar boy. I worked to keep the shock and disappointment invisible. I was simply a professional greeting a parent as I said, "Hi, Jon."

He smiled as he stood to greet me. "Hello again, An... Miss Melling," he finished with a glance at Ethan.

"I guess this means there's a new arrival," I said.

"Yeah, not until really late last night but they're both doing well."

"Congratulations on being a big brother, Ethan."

The boy smiled at me. He didn't say anything.

"Are you ready?" I asked him.

He grabbed my hand eagerly.

Jon said, "I just wait here, right?"

"Yeah. I'll bring him back as soon as we're done."

Jon nodded and took his seat again. He had a book with him. I led Ethan back and we went through a few typical activities. We ended with those frogs he liked.

"Okay, Ethan, we're going to do yucky or yummy. Here's your frog."

"I wanna boo one."

"All right, you can have blue." I traded frogs with him. "Now, let's see... how about ice cream? Yucky or yummy?"

"Ummy!"

"I think so, too. Hop your frog."

He gave his little plastic frog a hop closer to the center of the board and then looked up at me.

"Okay," I said. "What about pickles? Yucky or yummy?"

Ethan scrunched up his face as he said, "Ucky."

"Can you say it with an E like we practiced? Eee... yucky."

"Eee... ucky."

"I heard a Y in there. Good job. Give your frog a hop."

We went through several more foods before Ethan got his frog across the board. It was completely childish, but each time I asked the question I kept thinking that Jon was yummy and the fact that he was married was yucky. I completely understood Heather's annoyance at him for not wearing a ring.

I walked Ethan out to the main office. "He did very well today," I said to Jon.

"Good job, buddy." Jon held his hand out and Ethan slapped it.

"Has he met his new sister yet?"

"No, they won't let anyone under twelve visit at the hospital. I have a picture though. Want to see?" Jon pulled his phone out of his pocket while he was still talking. He held up a picture of a red-faced newborn wrapped in a pink blanket.

"Aw... she's cute. What's her name?"

"Valerie."

"That's pretty."

"Yeah, um... she and Heather have to stay at the hospital one more night. I thought maybe... well, you're probably still unpacking at your place... would you like to have dinner with me and Ethan?" He looked at Ethan before I could say anything. "Do you want Miss Melling to come over later?"

Ethan pressed his lips together tightly as he tried not to smile at the idea. He did give a tiny nod. Jon raised his eyes to me somewhat hesitantly. The pair of them were nearly irresistible. There was no way, however, that I was going to play house with

30

someone else's family. Just the thought of it squeezed my chest uncomfortably.

"No, thanks. I appreciate the offer, but…" I trailed off because I couldn't think of anything to say other than how much I just wanted them to leave.

"Okay," Jon said simply before he turned to Ethan. "Let's go, buddy."

Ethan said, "Wide!"

Jon crouched down and let the kid climb onto his back and walked out of the main office. I returned to mine and closed the door for a few deep breaths in private. I tried to console myself with the knowledge that even with his son there he would not have invited me over if he'd had any idea I'd been trying to flirt with him. It didn't help. I was still mortified to discover I'd let myself develop a crush on someone who was already married. I needed to be so much more careful. I didn't want anyone talking about my embarrassing love life, or embarrassing lack of a love life, while they bought cereal.

I decided in that moment that Parker and I had been hinting long enough. I knew my afternoon break overlapped with the time his class was out for their special. I made my way down the hall and stopped at the drinking fountain across from his open door.

"Hey, Angel," he said as he appeared in the doorway. "I thought that might be you."

"What can I say? I always need to stretch my legs this time of day. Those tiny kid chairs are brutal." I was not lying. I may not need to end up outside his classroom, but I did need a brief walk.

"Are we going to make a plan or what?"

I smiled as though I didn't understand. "What sort of plan?"

"Will you have dinner with me on Friday?"

"I will. Where do you want to go?"

He looked surprised. "No more playing around, huh?"

I shrugged. "If you don't want to…"

"Okay, I'll take you somewhere in the city."

"The city?"

"Port Harris. I know it's not really a city but compared to Hartford… anyway, should I pick you up at six or six-thirty?"

"Six is fine. Something casual?"

"Yes. I think this counts as a plan."

"I'll see you then."

31

He ducked back into his classroom and I returned to my office. I only had a few minutes before the next kid would arrive.

When I got home that day I spent a fair amount of time *looking* at the boxes all over my house. I couldn't bring myself to try any real unpacking. I didn't feel like doing anything at all so I sat in my living room and literally stared at the wall. I was trying to envision what the room should look like once I had everything in order.

The doorbell made me jump. I hadn't yet gotten used to the new chime. It was Riley Iverson.

"Hello, Riley." I greeted him as though I was happy to see him because he seemed to be an available man and I didn't know yet if I'd be happy to see him. It seemed like I should offer encouragement until I knew more about him even though he might have only stopped by for something to do with the house. My brain was stuck on looking for romantic intentions and occasionally imagining them as I had when I met Jon. All I really wanted at the moment was to not embarrass myself. That was a recurring theme in my life.

"Hi, uh... Angel." Riley looked at me and then towards the ground and then back at me. He appeared to be thinking about what to say.

"You're not here to evict me, are you?"

"No, I... no..." Riley smiled at my joke and blew out a quick breath before he began talking rapidly. "Dad, uh... Dad sent me over to make sure you're not having any problems with the mail because the last renter didn't get any for a while and it turned out to be his fault anyway so I doubt you would have messed that up but Dad thought I should check and I thought it wouldn't hurt to make sure." He looked at me as though he had asked a question and I suppose he sort of had.

"No problems. I started getting mail right away on Monday. Love how it comes right to the door." I gestured to the black mailbox to my left. It was rather old-fashioned with newspaper hooks on the bottom.

"Yeah," Riley said, "I live near the edge of town where the houses are newer and more spread out. Those are driving routes so we have to walk out to the curb."

I nodded. "That's the only way I've gotten mail in the past. Having the mailman come right on my porch is nice. But I suppose it's no fun to be the one lugging the bag of it."

Riley gave a tiny shrug and looked at the ground again. Then he said, "Also… Dad wanted me to ask you about the birds."

"What about the birds?"

He looked up towards the corner of the porch and talked while still facing that way. I followed his gaze as I listened. "They like to make nests in those corners under the roof and Dad usually knocks them down but if you'd like to watch for the babies then he would leave them alone. Though I guess they won't be back for several months still."

"I don't think I'd mind either way. Why does he knock them down?"

"They can be messy. They leave, um, droppings on the railings."

"Oh. Yeah, you can tell him to do whatever he wants."

"Okay." Riley looked back at me but his eyes kind of flicked around on my face. "Dad just thought… well, if he was going to be on the porch you might want some warning so it didn't startle you or if you wondered what he was doing or something."

It really was a good thing I was getting this warning in October that my landlord might at some point in the spring be on my porch. It was so obviously an excuse to see me. I was flattered. Perhaps I should decide to be happy to see Riley. I said, "Your dad doesn't seem scary so I think I'd have been okay."

"Yeah, he… he's a good guy, always talking to people."

"I did get the talker vibe from him but not… not from you so much?"

"It was annoying when we were kids. Seemed like every time we went somewhere we couldn't leave until Dad finished eight different conversations."

I smiled at him. "I can relate, though it was my mom who was always slowing the pace in my family. Especially at church. She always had to talk to a bunch of other people and I was always in a hurry to leave because we'd go out to lunch afterwards." My comment was intended to see if a mention of church affected him one way or the other. I was looking for a reason to rule him in or out as a romantic possibility.

He made a brief humming noise that sounded like understanding but really didn't communicate much to me. Then he scratched the side of his head. "I guess that's, um, that's all I needed."

"Are you sure?" I was giving him an opening to ask me out. I still didn't know if I was interested in the strong silent type but if he was interested in me then I was willing to give him a chance.

Riley nodded very slowly. "I think that's... yeah, I won't bother you anymore."

"It was no bother. Goodnight, I guess."

He nodded at me and quietly walked off my porch.

Chapter 6

I stopped by to see Parker again on Friday afternoon and he confirmed my address. I was a little excited about going out with him but not excited enough. I'm not sure how to describe it except that I was thinking about him as a date and not as a potential husband.

When I got home after work, I saw my empty trash can by the curb. I had remembered to put it out only after I got in my car and noticed all the cans along the street. Jeff had been taking care of that sort of thing the last few months. As I walked down to retrieve it, I felt a little sorry for myself for not having a husband I could send to the curb.

George was across the street walking his dog. I waved to him and he crossed to greet me. "Hi, Angel."

"George, thank you so much for the flowers. That was really nice of you."

"You're welcome. I'm glad you liked them."

I leaned over to give Mutt a few pats. "And thank you, too. I bet you helped pick them out, didn't you?"

"Mutt's always helpful."

"You said he was going to show me another trick."

"All right. Mutt, sit. Stay." George unhooked the leash and walked about ten steps ahead of Mutt, then he turned and patted his chest as he said, "Jump."

Mutt got a running start and hurled himself into George's arms. It was more cute than impressive but I cheered. George reattached the leash and walked Mutt back to me.

"That was great." I stroked Mutt's ear again. It was deliciously soft. "So, um…" I straightened and looked at George. I hadn't decided if he was too old for me. Too old meant someone who was not interested in giving me children, usually because he already had some without me. As far as I knew, George didn't have any

35

children so there was a chance that his age would make him in a hurry. That I could live with. "What do you do when you're not training Mutt for the circus?"

"I'm an insurance agent. My office is right here in town. It's one of those 'it pays the bills' sort of jobs."

I nodded. "I felt like that about some of the things I did in college and that was better than anything I could say about my last job. I'm pretty happy at Hartford Elementary… so far."

"I'm glad to hear that. Do you think you might be interested in telling me some specifics, like over dinner?"

"Will Mutt be there?"

"If you come to our house. You're not free tonight, are you?"

"I'm afraid I have plans. But tomorrow would work."

George smiled at me. "If you come over around five, you can play with Mutt while I cook."

"That's a very enticing offer. I'll be there."

"We'll be looking forward to it. Won't we, boy?"

I swear Mutt actually nodded at the question. I pet him one last time before I finished putting away my trash can and went into my house to change for my date with Parker, now the first of two dates in the same weekend. This was how to look for a husband. I needed to get out of my fantasy life and start spending time with available men.

It was a cool evening so I put on a bright red sweater with my jeans. I rarely wore makeup at school. I swiped on a hint of mascara and lip gloss to feel like I was making an effort.

Parker arrived in a shiny black BMW. The inside, however, was less shiny. The backseat was littered with fast food cups and wrappers. There was a stack of magazines and a couple of sweatshirts as well. I hoped the dark stain on the passenger seat was not sticky. I remembered how Jon said some of the cars he saw were pigsties and I wondered if he'd seen this one. As I closed the door I noticed a pickle smell. It made me think of Ethan and the face he made when he said pickles were yucky.

Parker started up the car and asked what I felt like eating.

"I sort of figured you had a place in mind," I said.

He shrugged. "I don't care. As long as it's not in Hartford."

"You don't think there are any good places to eat in Hartford?"

"There are exactly two but I… I don't need the gossip."

"Oh, I see… you're embarrassed to be seen with me."

He rolled his eyes. "It's not you. I just prefer a little privacy."

"I was only kidding."

He nodded slightly, but it didn't clear the tension that had suddenly appeared amidst the trash in his car. I simply looked at him for a minute. I guessed him to be in his early thirties. His hair was short and blond and he wore glasses with thin wire frames. He had a slightly paunchy stomach but wasn't really overweight.

"Have you been to Daniel's?" I asked. "It's an Italian place on State Street."

"Yeah, that sounds fine. So, um, do you have any hobbies?"

"I read a lot but otherwise not really." I paused for a moment, hoping he wasn't going to ask what I read. A lot of it was romantic fiction or marriage advice. I liked to dream about my happily ever after and when I found a husband I was going to be deliriously happy. It was only fair that I prepared to do my best to return the favor. Parker Jones did not need to know that. "What about you?" I asked. I thought we should stick to discussing hobbies.

"Uhh… sometimes I build models."

"Like cars?"

"Mostly."

"Does that involve painting and stuff or just putting them together?"

"I paint them."

Our conversation was nearly as dull as my lack of hobbies. I couldn't think of anything else to say.

Parker said, "I know you have a sister. Any other siblings?"

"No, just the two of us. But I like Jeff and I'm looking forward to a niece or nephew so the family is getting bigger."

I couldn't see his eyes because he was facing the road. Something told me they had rolled into his head again. "I suppose you want to help make your family bigger?"

"You mean have my own kids?"

He nodded.

I said, "Eventually." Because "as soon as possible" felt like a bad answer at the time.

"I don't get that," he said. "You're around kids all day."

"Other people's kids. That's not the same thing."

"It's better."

"Are you telling me that an elementary school teacher doesn't like kids?"

"Don't get me wrong. I like kids just fine. At school. I also like coming home to peace and quiet. Besides, kids are expensive."

I did not comment on the number of diapers a person could buy for the cost of the car he was driving. I was trying to guess what the odds were that his class just got on his nerves a whole bunch that day. Because if he really didn't want kids, then we might as well cancel the rest of the date.

We were both quiet, and a little tense. Eventually he flipped on the radio. He turned it up loud enough that talking would have been difficult and I felt relieved. We pulled into the restaurant parking lot and Parker smiled at me as we got out of the car. The smile looked only partially forced.

We were given a small table near the front of the restaurant. Neither of us spoke while we examined our menus. Once we had ordered, I attempted to start a conversation with the first thing that popped into my head. "We passed St. Christopher's only a block from here. I'll be there Sunday morning. Do you go to church?"

He shrugged. "Well, I'm Catholic but when I go I usually go to the Methodist church in Hartford because it's closer."

"That doesn't make any sense."

"Why not?"

"It's like saying you're a fifth grader, but you go to a first grade classroom. They're different."

"The Methodist church plays better music."

"Music? You shouldn't pick a church based on superficial things like music or which one has a better nursery."

"I won't need a nursery anyway."

I think he was trying to make a joke, trying to derail what was almost a full-blown argument. Reminding me of something else we didn't have in common made me something close to angry. "And the fact that you're willing to drive to Port Harris for dinner but not for worship says that-"

"Don't get all pious on me," he said to cut me off. "I don't need a lecture." His voice had as much edge to it as mine.

I took a deep breath. I was not angry at Parker. I was angry that we weren't clicking and that was as much my fault as his. We both knew the evening was a mistake and there was no point making it worse. "I'm sorry," I said. "What did you order again?"

He let me change the subject and we chatted about the food options until our dinner arrived. I don't know how fast he normally ate, but he practically inhaled his pasta and I was not offended. I was happy that we could leave as soon as I was finished. He turned on the radio in the car as soon as he started it. The drive back to Hartford was not too bad. We listened to music and not each other.

****

Saturday morning I did some serious unpacking. I had spent most of the week getting things out as I needed them and my house was still a mess of boxes. I managed to get the kitchen in pretty good shape by lunchtime and worked to hang up some clothes in the afternoon. Eventually I got bored of being productive so I took a shower and let my hair air-dry while I read a few chapters in my latest novel. If Charlotte didn't end up with Jason I was going to be so mad.

My house was quiet and I heard footsteps on my porch. There was a fairly long pause before the doorbell chimed. It was Riley again. I smoothed my hair before I opened the door.

"Hi, Riley. Here to evict me this time?"

He let out a short, self-conscious laugh. "Not this time either. I, um… well, Dad sent me again."

"Do you work with your dad? Helping with properties and stuff?"

"Not usually. He only rents this one place."

"But he likes to send you on errands?"

The big guy at my door seemed to shrink as he shrugged and nodded at the same time.

"So today you…" I prompted.

"Dad wants to mow the lawn on Monday and he wants to know if that would cause you any trouble."

Bill and I had already talked about lawn mowing and how I didn't care when he took care of it. I attempted a bit of teasing. "What if it rains Monday? What's the alternate grass cutting day?"

Riley's eyes got a bit more round just before he hid them behind his full lashes. "Uh… he didn't… or I didn't ask. I thought, or hoped you wouldn't mind whenever…" He shifted his weight. "I can call if…"

"No, I'm kidding," I said. "I thought your dad already knew that I'm completely open to whatever yard work schedule he likes. Between reasonable daylight hours anyway."

"Yeah, I thought… that's good." Riley looked at me again. "So you like the house? Still no problems?"

"It's still wonderful and I still have your card if something comes up." Maybe that's why he was hesitating. Maybe the ball was in my court. Maybe I needed to hint that I was open to this possibility in front of me. "But I'm still learning the ins and outs of Hartford," I said. "Can you think of anything I should know?"

He looked thoughtful but then shook his head.

"Anywhere I should go?"

That question was met with a completely vacant expression.

"I mean, if I wanted to go out and do something interesting what might be a good place to visit."

He drew a slow breath. "We don't… Hartford is quiet, dull to some people. I like the calm."

I nodded. "Yeah, I don't really mean a nightclub or anything. Just a quiet meal."

"I like Fred's." He clamped his lips together as though he regretted the words and there might have been a faint blush creeping out from under his collar.

"I think I saw that place. Fred's Fine Food?"

He tipped his head up and down, sort of like a reluctant nod, and then looked over his shoulder. "I guess, um, if you don't need anything else right now…"

"Thanks for checking on me."

"Bye," he said softly as he slouched off my porch. I was a bit disappointed that he didn't ask me out. I still didn't know if I liked him, but it was starting to feel as though a full date was the only way I'd be able to form an opinion.

Chapter 7

I waited until a few minutes after five to walk across the street for my second date of the weekend. A relationship with a near neighbor could be very convenient, if I ended up with one. There were a few barks when I knocked on the door. Then I heard George's voice. I couldn't tell what he said, but Mutt must have understood because he quieted.

"Come on in," George said as he opened the door. "There are some hooks there." He pointed to a coat rack by the door. I took off my light jacket and hung it and my purse on one of the hooks. "Let me show you around some." George took me through the living room, which had a large TV and some astronomy books on the coffee table. He pointed out a bathroom in case I needed one and showed me the dining room. He'd already set the table with candles. There were old black and white photographs on the walls, the kind where no one smiled.

"These are cool," I said. "Family members?"

"I believe I'm related to all of them, but there are a few where I don't know the exact connection. My grandmother was a genealogy buff. I got these when she died a few years ago."

"Oh, I'm sorry."

He acknowledged the sentiment with a nod. "This one is her mother. This one is my grandmother with all six of her siblings."

"Do you have siblings?"

"No. Do you?"

"Just one sister. She lives in Port Harris."

George smiled slightly. "I called it by name when I first moved here, too. I think I've mostly taken to calling it 'the city' like everyone else."

"It's probably not the only way I stick out."

"You stick out in a good way."

A compliment. So far the evening was feeling very polite, but it was an improvement over my last date. "Thank you," I said.

George led me into the kitchen and asked if I liked stir fry.

"Yeah, that sounds good."

"Are you vegetarian or allergic to something or anything else someone cooking for you should know?"

I shook my head. "As far as I know I can eat anything."

"I think Mutt can relate to that." George looked down at his dog, who had been quietly following the tour. I knelt to pet him. His dark brown eyes closed halfway as he enjoyed the attention.

"I have a lot of chopping to do," George said. "If you want, you can take Mutt into the backyard for a while. It's fenced so he can run around."

"That sounds fun." I went back and grabbed my jacket and met Mutt and George by the back door. George opened it. Mutt waited for permission before he darted outside. George pointed out a plastic box near the door.

"There are some toys in there. He's really good with a Frisbee."

I nodded and followed Mutt. He was better with a Frisbee than I was. The first time I threw it he sprinted ahead and had to backtrack a bit to catch it. After a few tosses he figured out that I was not going to be throwing it as far as George apparently did. I was so impressed with the little guy's jumps. Mutt had amazing air time. I was afraid of wearing him out too much though. When he slowed down somewhat, I sat on the steps. He sat next to me and put his head in my lap. I'm not sure how long I sat there stroking him, but it was the first time in a long time that I felt completely content. He was a great dog.

"Did you both get tired?" George's voice behind me made me jump. Mutt also jumped up and stood at the door to be let inside.

"I hope he had as much fun as I did," I said as I stood. There was a delicious food smell coming through the back door. "Is it time to eat?"

George nodded and let me and Mutt inside. I hung up my jacket again and washed my hands while he put dinner on the table. He lowered his head and we each said a silent prayer before he offered me the serving spoon. I helped myself to some rice and a wonderful mix of beef and vegetables. "This is great," I said as soon as I swallowed my first bite.

"Thank you."

I noticed Mutt lying in a corner near the table. He was stretched out as though he might take a nap, but his eyes were *very* alert. They were taking in every move that George made.

"Did you train Mutt yourself? I mean not just the tricks. I don't think I've ever seen a dog with better manners."

"Yeah, I put a lot of time into him. He even worked as a therapy dog for a few years at the hospital in the city. We took a break that I meant to be temporary, but we just haven't gotten it back into our schedule."

"I bet he was the most popular one."

"I don't think he got tired of the attention."

"How did you get him to not beg at the table?"

"Patience mostly. He knows now that I always save the last bite for him. If he's good, I'll bring it to him when I'm done."

I nodded and enjoyed a few bites myself.

"You seem to really like dogs," George said. "Have you thought about getting one of your own?"

"Sort of."

"Sort of?"

"It's always been part of the plan. First I finish school. Then I get married and have a couple of kids. After a few years the kids start bugging me to get a dog and I let them think they talked me into it."

George laughed. "Interesting plan."

"Yes, it's been working out *very* well for me. But you know what they say… we plan and God laughs."

"I've heard that. And I suspect I've given Him a few chuckles myself over the years."

"I certainly never planned on moving to Hartford. I followed my sister to Port Harris and intended to stay there. I interviewed at a place there and another applicant told me she had heard of a job in Hartford and I was like 'Where's Hartford?' Now I live here and well, it feels right."

"Hartford does have its downsides. But I don't think I'm going anywhere."

We finished the meal with light conversation. Mutt sat up as soon as George pushed back his chair. The dog eagerly took the bite of meat he was offered and followed us into the kitchen as we cleared the table. George said he would take care of most of the cleanup later and we sat in his living room for a while. Mutt was invited onto the couch and he positioned himself between us. I didn't stay very long. George walked me to the door and we said, "Goodnight," almost as though we were old friends. It hit me about halfway down the sidewalk that acting like old friends was probably not a romantic beginning.

****

I woke up the next morning and lay in bed thinking about Mutt's soft fur and adoring eyes. Disappointment set in when I realized I was not thinking about George at all. Maybe this would be one of those things that developed slowly. Maybe that's what God had been trying to tell me when He threw the married guy into my path. I needed to slow down.

I got up and got ready for church. St. Christopher's was a fairly large parish. I'm not very good at estimating, but I think at least 600 people could sit in the pews. I had been sitting on the far right, near the choir. I decided as I entered to try the left side. Even though I had told myself I was going to wait to see if something happened with George or maybe Riley, I knew I wanted to sit on a different side to look at different people... different guys.

As I walked up the aisle I spotted someone who was not different. Jon was seated at the end of a pew. Ethan was standing on the seat next to him. I recognized Caitlin somewhere in the middle of the row before I turned around. There was apparently a whole clan of Thorpes over there. I went to the right side and simply sat closer to the back than usual.

I was mostly surrounded by families and much older couples. I noticed a man two rows ahead of me though who might have been alone. There was a girl next to him who looked about nine or ten, but there was a family on her other side and I couldn't tell if she belonged with them or not. Then I told myself to pay attention. I was not at church to look for a man. That was worse than going for the music.

I did succeed in focusing for a while. When we turned to pass the peace though, the man I'd noticed reached across the pew between us to shake my hand. That felt significant.

As people began to leave, I cut him off in the aisle to introduce myself. "Hi," I said and held out my hand. "I'm Angel Melling. I'm pretty new here. Have you been a member for long?"

He said, "A few years," as he took my hand briefly.

Then I realized that the girl was evidently with him and that he was wearing a wedding band. She seemed to be in a hurry to leave and I just stood there awkwardly feeling sure that it was obvious that the wedding band was the reason I had nothing else to say. Both the man and the girl tried to smile at me as they moved past. My face was completely hot and I sat down to put some distance between us. I'm not sure if the tear that worked its way out of my eye was due to embarrassment or frustration. I thought I had resolved to be less reckless. I pushed it off my check as a soft voice next to me said, "Are you okay?"

I looked up and felt warmer. Jon was standing next to me.

"I'm sorry," he said. "That was a dumb question. I meant is there anything… do you need anything other than to be left alone?"

"I'm fine," I said. It was almost convincing.

He nodded and left quickly. What had started as a promising weekend was not going well. I stopped and visited with Jeff and Ashley for almost two hours though and that was nice. I called my parents later in the afternoon and they were happy to hear from me. That was nice, too.

Chapter 8

Heather was back on Monday and was surrounded by nearly all the women in the office cooing and fussing over tiny Valerie. Ethan seemed fairly indifferent to the commotion, but I still tried to focus my attention on him. I pulled out some dot paint in my office and let him mark pictures of the words he said. I offered my congratulations to Heather as she left and I did steal a peek at the baby.

Caitlin came to my office for lunch. We sat at the short table while we ate. She had barely unwrapped her sandwich when she said, "Okay, here's the thing. My brother Jon said that he saw you at church and that you looked upset. He made me promise to find out if there was anything really wrong so this is me asking if there's anything wrong."

Caitlin had dark hair like her brother and the same light blue eyes. Despite her cheery tone, those eyes showed genuine concern so I decided to be honest. Or at least vaguely honest.

"Please don't give him the details. I just… I had a rather lousy date this weekend and I was sort of having a little pity party for myself. No one needs to be worried about me."

"I should fix you up with my brother," she said.

I shook my head. I planned to remember that at least one of her brothers was single. But at the moment, I did not need to be fixed up with anyone who would make me think of Jon. "I'm not sure I need help," I said.

"There's nothing wrong with a little help. Someone needs to help my sister Emma, that's for sure."

"What's going on with her," I asked, trying to keep the topic flowing away from me.

"She likes this guy named Jimmy Larrick. They were in the same class in high school and he asked her out and she wasn't interested then. They've been spending some time together now

46

with mutual friends and she totally has a thing for him and won't say anything because she once turned him down, you know, years ago. Someone needs to tell those two they make a cute couple."

It was easy for a married person to say something like that. Caitlin was nice though. She only wanted others to be as happy as she was with Dan... most of the time.

"How did the carpet shopping go?" I asked.

Caitlin's eyes bugged out. "Oh, my goodness! I don't know who I married. He wants shag."

"Shag carpeting?"

"It's this horrible tomato red. Dan has lost his mind and there's no way I'm putting that in our bedroom. We agreed not to discuss it for a week. He actually thinks I'm going to change my mind if I think about it. I wouldn't change my mind if I had years to think about it."

"So you're moving on to the paint selection?"

Caitlin shook her head. "I think we're just going to clean up some of the other projects for a bit."

I told Caitlin that was probably a good idea. I wasn't in a position to give advice, but it wasn't advice so much as support.

****

I stopped at the Market after work and kept my eyes open for Jon. If Monday was his regular shopping day, I wanted to see him before he saw me so I could hopefully avoid him. I didn't see anyone I recognized until I reached the checkout line. "Hi, Mabel."

"Hi, hon. Angel, right?"

I nodded as I began to unload my groceries.

"I hear you got a nice welcome. Flowers from a certain eligible man?"

"It was a nice welcome. Very neighborly."

"Neighborly?" Mabel smirked at my word choice. "You gonna be one of those private types?"

"I think I'd share if I had something to share."

"The last person who told me that showed up with an engagement ring like two weeks later."

"I would definitely bet against me having an engagement ring two weeks from now." My eyes involuntarily floated over my naked left hand as I said it.

Mabel appeared for a moment to be considering the odds on the bet. She said, "Well, I have news. One of my nephews just had his second baby last week. A girl."

"As a matter of fact, I met Valerie this morning. I work with Ethan at school."

"Oh, that's right. Isn't Ethan the sweetest little boy?"

"He's adorable," I said. "And I would say that even if he wasn't related to you."

Mabel nodded approvingly and I paid for my groceries. I took them out to the parking lot and continued to watch for anyone I might want to avoid. I had just closed my trunk when I spotted Jon stepping out of a car a few rows ahead of me. I left the cart where it was and jumped into my car before he could see me. I made a mental note to switch my shopping day to Tuesday the next week as I watched him enter the store. Then I got back out to put the cart away and climbed behind the wheel to turn the key.

Nothing happened. Well, something happened, but the engine starting was not it. The dash lights flashed for a moment before they went out. I turned the key again and got only a faint clicking noise. My battery was dead. I had jumper cables and I had actually used them once before. I still needed a second car and someone willing to let me use it. I also needed to know where I could get a new battery. Mabel would know. She'd probably know which employee would let me use his or her car as well.

I stuffed my keys in my purse and went back inside. Jon was not in sight and Mabel was just finishing with a customer. She saw me approaching. "Hi, hon. Did you forget something?"

"Not exactly. The battery on my car is dead and I wondered if someone could-"

"Oh, hon, don't worry. I just saw Jonathon. He'll take care of that for you."

I'm not sure how I could have said that I would have preferred someone else, anyone else, to come to my rescue. But she didn't even look at me before she picked up a phone next to her register. "Summer," she said into it, "Jonathon just came in. Can you call him up here for me?"

She hung up and a few seconds later a female voice came over the intercom and said, "Attention Jonathon Thorpe, someone at the front of the store cannot go another second without your company. Please report to register two for details."

In twenty-eight years I had never wanted a rock to hide under more than I did at that moment. I may not have been the only one. Jon walked up to Mabel's other side saying, "For crying out loud, Mabel, you could have just called me." He picked up the same phone she had and said, "Very funny, Summer." He clearly hung up without waiting for any response and then he appeared to be about to say something else to Mabel when he saw me. He pressed his mouth shut.

Mabel said, "Jon, dear, this is Angel Melling. She's having some car trouble and I knew you'd be able to help her out."

"Yes, ma'am," he said to his aunt, who looked delighted. He didn't really look at me as he jerked his head to indicate I should follow him outside.

I began to apologize as soon as I thought we were out of Mabel's hearing range. "I'm so sorry about that. I had no idea... I just... My battery died and I asked her if she knew who'd be willing to give me a jump."

Jon nodded and I think he was trying not to smile. "Don't worry about it. I do happen to know how to use jumper cables. Where are you parked?"

We had just gotten outside and I pointed to my car. I didn't trust my voice not to be squeaky. I was too nervous. My brain knew he was off limits. My body still felt warm and uncoordinated around him.

"Oh, I see it," he said. "Go over there and wait while I move my car."

I nodded and did as I was told. Fortunately, the space right across from my car was open. I handed him my keys and stood back while he worked. When the cars were running and unhooked, he came up to me. "Follow me to the garage and I'll put in a new battery for you."

"But you're off now," I said. "You can just tell me where it is."

He shook his head. "I know you have a trunk full of groceries. I want to make sure you don't have to wait."

I didn't want to let him be nice to me, but I couldn't make him tell me where to go so I said, "Okay," and got in my car.

The Hartford Garage was barely outside of town. We made only one turn and drove until the buildings thinned. It would not have been difficult for Jon to give me that information. He parked first and I pulled in next to him. He signaled for me to pop the

49

hood before I got out. Then he took off his jacket and tossed it onto his passenger seat through the open window. "I'll be right back," he said.

There were two garage doors on the left side of the building. One was open and one was closed. There was an automotive parts store on the right side and that's where Jon entered. A minute later, a different man came out through the open garage door wearing the same navy work shirt. He looked significantly older. "Good day, ma'am," he said. "Can I help you with something?"

"Thank you, but someone is already helping me."

He looked confused for a moment, but then Jon came out carrying a battery. "Hey, Jon," he said. "What are you doing back?"

Jon looked again like he was biting back a smile. "A voice from above told me I was needed."

The older man furrowed his brow again.

"I'll tell you about it later, Dad."

"I look forward to a fascinating story." The man, who was apparently Jon's dad, reached into his pocket and pulled out a small folded card. He walked over and handed it to me. "Here's a little customer comment card. If he screws up at all, feel free to describe the mistake in great detail on here and then leave it inside." He winked at me as he left.

Jon called, "Thanks a lot, Dad," to his retreating back.

I stepped a little closer to watch Jon change the battery. He didn't say anything and seemed anxious, almost as anxious as I felt. I tried to think of a reason and thought he might have realized after the fact that inviting me over while his wife was not home could have been misconstrued. I took a step backward to make sure he didn't think that. He finished quickly and charged me only for the cost of the battery. I thanked him as profusely as I could without gushing before I drove home, still planning to buy groceries on a different day the next week.

Chapter 9

Tuesday afternoon I stretched my legs past a few fourth grade rooms. I waved through the open door to Parker, who waved back. Neither of us said anything. I was trying to be very mature about the situation while also pretending that I had *not* been walking down that hallway only to get him to ask me out. It was a fine line.

I had scrambled eggs for dinner and sat down with a book. Through the window I saw George leave his house with Mutt. I grabbed a jacket and went outside to ask if he'd mind some company.

"Not at all," he said.

I gave Mutt a quick pat and fell into step next to them.

"How was work today?" George asked.

"Pretty good. I saw this little girl today... she's one of the older ones and comes to me because of a stutter. I guess she had trouble saying something in class yesterday and another little girl laughed at her. Before the teacher could even say something, a boy behind them told the other little girl to 'shut up because it's not funny.' Oh, my... the way she told me about this boy standing up for her... I think she's planning a wedding already."

George sighed. "That little boy is in trouble."

"I think it's sweet."

"It's sweet unless she tells people. Then the teasing begins."

"Sounds like maybe this kid can take it. I do hope it's not a problem for either of them though."

"Do all girls start planning weddings when they're what? Ten?"

"No," I said. Some of them wait until they're twenty-eight and then go nuts trying to make up for lost time. "How's your week starting out?"

"Fine I guess. I don't think I have any stories."

"Does Mutt want to do another trick for me?"

George stopped and appeared to give this some thought. I think he was only trying to decide which trick Mutt wanted to show me. "Sit," he said. "Stay." George slowly backed up and laid the leash on the sidewalk between him and Mutt. Then he held his finger out like a gun and said, "Bang!" Mutt sort of drooped to the side and slowly rolled so that all four of his legs stuck up.

"Good boy," George said as he picked up the leash with one hand and used the other to ruffle Mutt's fur.

"That was awesome. How did you get him to wilt like that?"

"That's all him. I tried to teach him to fall over quickly, but he just insisted on doing it slowly. He's a natural ham I guess."

I felt the soft fuzz of Mutt's ears for a moment before we continued our walk. He had earned it. George and I talked about the weather getting cooler and the leaves changing color. I didn't have a brother, but talking to him felt sort of like talking to Jeff. I wondered if it had something to do with the age difference. He had told me on Saturday that he was forty-one. I didn't think that was too old, but the only other explanation I could think of was that I was too hung up on Jon to consider anyone else. And that was ridiculous. George and I just needed more time together.

When we had almost returned to my house I said, "I think I owe you a dinner now. Would you like to come to my house on Saturday? Mutt can come. You'd have to forgive a few boxes though. I'm not completely organized."

He agreed and we settled on a time before we reached my sidewalk. We had a cordial parting. I returned to my book wishing that I was looking forward to Saturday more.

****

I kind of freaked out on Wednesday. I believe, or rather I really hope and pray, that I kept the freak out completely internal. I only know that Caitlin did not show any signs of me acting weird.

The day began normally. I saw a few kids from the school and then Ethan came in. I introduced him to a new game that I think he liked about as much as the frogs. After he left, I printed a note about our session in his file before I put it away and a name caught my eye. On a line next to father, the form said "Thomas."

That was strange. It couldn't be a typo. Was Jonathon a middle name? I flipped through the file and found that every form listed

Ethan's parents as Thomas and Heather Thorpe. There was no mention of a middle name or even a middle initial.

I needed an explanation and I knew Caitlin could help with that. I wasn't sure how to bring it up casually though. She sat with me for lunch and I let her talk about some sort of computer problem they were having. "It freezes up at the worst times and then the IT guy keeps looking at me like I did something."

"Are you sure you didn't?" I teased.

"Everything I don't do now I just have to do later."

"I know. Did you tell him that?"

"It wasn't worth explaining. I'm crossing my fingers that it's all fixed for the afternoon."

"Good." I took a bite of my sandwich, trying not to look distracted while trying to think of a way to get her to talk about her family.

"Leslie had a busy morning."

"Nothing serious I hope." Leslie was the nurse.

Caitlin shook her head. "Two bloody noses and a kid who complained that his foot hurt. Eventually she figured out that he had been sitting on it."

"That's not so bad."

"In my opinion, anything that doesn't involve someone throwing up is not so bad."

I tried to look as though I agreed. "I like that sweater, by the way."

"Thanks. I borrowed it from Emma."

There was my opening. "I know Emma is younger than you and you also have three brothers, right?"

She nodded.

"Are they all older or... where do you fit in?"

Caitlin put down her fork and prepared to describe her family. I prepared to listen attentively.

"Tommy is the oldest," she said. "You know him because he's Ethan's dad."

I nodded even though I was not convinced I knew anything of the sort.

"Christopher is next. He's twenty-nine and lives in Tennessee. He met someone while he was in college and followed her to her hometown when they got married. They already have three kids. He comes home at least for Christmas. I'm right in the middle and you know all about me." She paused to flash a big grin. "Emma's the baby and Jon is between us." She looked as though she wanted to say something else. I thought she had already said almost everything. Jon and Tommy were two different people and only one of them was married to Heather. Did that mean that Jon was single after all!?

I looked at the sandwich I was eating and concentrated on staying perfectly calm. Maybe he was seeing someone else. Caitlin answered my unasked question and made staying calm rather difficult. She said, "So I know you met Jon a few times and he's really nice and I want to fix you guys up and I think you should say yes so *please* think about it."

I glanced up and her expression said that she thought she was asking me a big favor. I bit the side of my lower lip in an attempt to appear uncertain. "Do you really think that's a good idea?"

She nodded hopefully. "Is it because he's younger than you? He'll be twenty-five next month so it's not like it's a *big* difference. We'll do it on Friday. Let me text Dan to make sure we don't have plans I'm forgetting about." She pulled out her phone and punched in a message before she continued working on me. "You and Jon can come to our house and it'll be real casual and… I'll make something good to eat so you'll at least get a free meal out of it."

"This Friday?" I asked.

She shrugged. "Why wait?"

"I have to admit I don't have anything else going on."

"Perfect. You just keep Friday open and I'll get Jon to come and take care of everything."

Sorry, Ashley. Caitlin was now my new best friend.

****

If she hadn't looked so determined, Caitlin might have had to relinquish that best friend title the next day. She popped into my office first thing and said, "My brother is an idiot."

"Is there a problem?"

Caitlin sighed heavily and leaned against the door frame. "He won't come," she said. "He said he didn't know what kind of arm-twisting I did to get you to agree but that there was no way I was going to talk him into it." She sighed again. "He doesn't understand that I'm trying to help. And I *will* think of a way." She pointed a pen she was holding toward me. "So you're off the hook for Friday, but I expect you to go along when I think of a good plan."

"You sound a little nuts," I told her.

"Someday you will both thank me." She smiled at me and then left.

Caitlin was a little crazy, but so was I. I'd been replaying every moment with Jon in my head, trying to figure out who I could blame for my confusion. I decided it was easiest to be mad at Heather. If she hadn't specifically said that her husband was bringing Ethan, I would not have necessarily made that leap. I'd have clarified. I'd have said something like, "I didn't know Ethan was your son," or "Why didn't you tell me I'd been working with your son?" I'd have given Jon a chance to tell me that he was babysitting. Then I'd have had a chance to see him as I did now... a good-looking man who seemed to like kids and who went to my church and whose dinner invitation might not have been entirely neighborly. Now that was a serious prospect. And I turned him down!

Chapter 10

I was restless all day, thinking about how I had screwed up. Even if Caitlin came through for me in arranging something, I was likely going to have to make some sort of move. And that would probably need to involve me explaining my mistake. I'd introduced myself to plenty of guys recently, tried to give them an opening, but I still waited for them to express real interest first.

I went for a walk after my dinner. I wasn't sure whether or not I was hoping to bump into George. I wouldn't mind a friendly chat. So far things had been only friendly between us. The flowers, however, hinted that he might try to change that. I wasn't in the mood for some sort of relationship-defining talk. What I think I really wanted was to bump into Mutt out walking by himself. I could absolutely go for that kind of simple companionship.

I walked the same direction I had walked with my neighbor earlier in the week, but when I got back to my house I still didn't feel like going inside. I walked past the house and soon reached that darker blue one that George had mentioned the day we met. There was an older couple sitting on a white porch swing.

The woman said, "Hey, Walt, it's our new neighbor."

The man said, "Get her up here already."

Then the woman called out to me. "Sweetheart! Come on up here and introduce yourself. We've been dying to meet our new neighbor."

I remembered George's warning but didn't have anything else to do so I walked up the sidewalk. I stopped at the bottom of the porch steps and was about to say my name when the woman jumped – she appeared more agile than I expected – off the swing and motioned me closer. "No, no, all the way up. Take this seat right here." She pointed to a white rocking chair across from the swing and on the other side of their front door. She claimed a second rocker closer to the steps. I could see how I'd be strategically tucked between her and the front of the house and how a graceful exit might be challenging. I sat anyway.

"My name is Angel Melling," I said.

The woman nodded and yelled to her husband, "Angel."

"What's that?" he asked.

"Her name is Angel." When he continued the blank stare she said, "Like in the song." She began to sing "Angels We Have Heard on High." She had a lovely voice and got halfway through the chorus before he nodded.

I had no idea what he thought he understood.

The woman turned back to me. "I'm Carol and that's Walt. We've been married fifty-three years."

"Congratulations." I didn't know if that meant they were celebrating an anniversary or simply liked to brag.

"You moved from the city?" Carol asked.

"I did."

"You like Hartford?"

"Yeah, so far."

Walt said, "Ask her how she likes Hartford."

Carol waved off the question. I nodded at Walt to answer him. Carol said, "Are you married?"

"No."

"Don't you worry, sweetheart. Hartford has tons of eligible bachelors."

"I think I only need one."

She smiled at me. "That's right. You just find the right one and settle down."

"Gloria," Walt said, "what grade do you teach down there at the school?"

"Um…" I glanced at Carol, who didn't seem to notice that he thought my name was Gloria. "I'm a speech therapist." I said it as loudly as I could without shouting.

"A gymnast? You mean like the gym teacher?"

"She said a speech therapist," Carol said. She *was* shouting.

Walt nodded. "Do the kids like that?"

"I think they enjoy it. I try to make it fun."

He nodded again. It didn't look as though he actually heard me.

Carol put her hand on my arm. "Bill was so happy you agreed to let him take care of the lawn."

"It makes me happy, too." When we discussed the lease, he offered me a discount if I would let him do all the yard work. I didn't know if he was a marketing genius who'd started with an inflated rent or simply a man who enjoyed cutting grass. It felt like a good deal to me either way.

"He'll do a good job for you," Carol said.

"The grass is already shorter."

"Gloria, do you think you could do me a favor?"

This was why she hadn't corrected her husband. "My name is Angel," I said.

"Oh, that's right. I'm sorry, dear."

"It's okay. What favor did you need?"

"Can you reach up there and tighten that light bulb 'til it comes on?" She pointed to a light near the door.

I stood and turned the bulb. It lit quickly. As I returned to my seat I asked if the switch was broken.

Carol shook her head and looked as though she didn't understand why I had asked. I don't think Walt knew what I said. He said, "I made those chairs myself."

I gave mine an extra rock. "I'm impressed."

He nodded proudly and said, "Ask her if she plays Gin."

"Gloria, do you play Gin?" Carol said it as though the idea had just occurred to her.

"I have, but it's been a while. I might not remember."

"Get the cards," Carol said to her husband before she acknowledged my response. "We'll show you, dear. It's easy."

Walt opened the door and reached inside to where a deck of cards and a notepad was waiting on a little table. He pulled the whole table onto the porch while his wife refreshed my memory on the rules of Gin.

I was beginning to plan my exit after several hands. But as Carol shuffled the cards for what we'd agreed would be the last round, she said, "Walt, get the pictures."

He was in the house for at least five minutes and came out with a black photo album. He held it on his lap while we played that last hand. Then he opened the book on the table so that he was looking at it upside-down and Carol could narrate the contents to me. They had seven grandchildren and two great-grandchildren in the pictures. The order was not chronological so that someone who was ten years old in one picture looked about two on the next

58

page. I was not going to keep them straight, but Carol and Walt did not appear to be setting me up for a quiz.

About halfway through the pages Carol said, "Oh, wait… this is the wrong book. I wanted to show you the most recent ones."

"These are wonderful. You can show me the others later."

Carol nodded but she yelled, "Get the blue one," to Walt before she began telling me about the next picture.

I forced myself to yawn a few times. I was planning on letting her finish the first album and then insisting that I was simply too tired for another one. Carol seemed to be turning the pages slower and slower though as if she sensed my escape plan.

A young man I'd never seen before walked up to the porch before we finished. "Good evening, Carol… Walt."

"Why, hello, Seth. How are you today, young man?" Carol greeted him.

Walt said, "We'll make room for Carol to show you the pictures."

The young man – his name might have been Seth but mine wasn't Gloria so I wasn't sure – looked at Carol. "I'm just fine," he said, "but Jill's visiting and she's having some sort of girl problem and I hoped I could borrow our new neighbor to help her out."

"Oh, of course." Carol moved the album off the table to give me some room. "You go see what Jill needs," she said to me.

I jumped up, happy enough to be leaving that I wasn't too concerned with the fact that my exit didn't make much sense. I waved to the older couple.

"Goodnight, Gloria," Carol called.

The newcomer grinned at me almost as soon as I was off the porch and said, "You're welcome."

I walked down the sidewalk with him. "Why am I thanking you and who are you?"

He laughed. "You know why you're thanking me. I'm Seth. Didn't you hear that?"

"Didn't you hear them call me Gloria?"

"I did. Nice to meet you Gloria."

"My name isn't Gloria."

I didn't know where we were going, but at this point we were in the middle of the street. Seth stopped – in the middle of the street – and turned to face me. "Why did you tell them your name is Gloria if it isn't?"

"I didn't."

"Well, what is your name?"

"Angel."

Seth nodded seriously and said, "I guess that does sound exactly like Gloria," with heavy sarcasm. Then he gestured for me to continue following him across the street. "Come meet Jill for a minute so they think you're helping her with something."

"Who is Jill?" I asked.

"My sister."

When he didn't say girlfriend or wife, I checked him out a bit more closely. The first thing I noticed was the absence of a wedding ring. Unfortunately, I no longer knew what that meant. I used to think that meant a guy wasn't married. But then I found out that some married guys didn't always wear their rings and that if I thought someone who wasn't wearing a ring was married he might actually *not* be married.

The next thing I noticed was the air of confidence. Seth walked like a guy who doubted nothing, a guy who knew that a complete stranger would follow him across the street if he suggested it. He was only a little taller than me and had sun-streaked blond hair. He was wearing shorts and a red T-shirt. His outfit made me zip my jacket.

I realized that he was taking me to a small apartment building not directly across the street from where we'd started. There were two units on the first floor and two on the second. A woman with jet black curly hair was standing in front of one of the lower apartments. She was wearing red and pink striped knee socks under a black dress. As we reached her I realized it was a maternity dress.

"That was fast," she said.

"I'm good," Seth answered.

"I'm Jill," the woman said to me.

"Angel."

She tipped her head forward. "Nice to meet you, Angel. I noticed you sitting with Walt and Carol when I got here so when I realized you were still over there as I was leaving I thought one of us should do something."

"By one of us," Seth said, "she meant me."

"What did you say to get her out of there?"

He shrugged. "I said you were having some sort of girl problem."

"What sort of girl problem?" Jill looked at me for clarification.

I said, "That's it. He came over there and said, 'Jill is having some sort of girl problem.'"

"What does that mean?" She looked back at her brother.

He shrugged again. "They're nice. I knew they'd let her leave if I used the word problem and it had to be something I couldn't help with."

Jill playfully punched Seth in the arm. "What if they ask me about this imaginary and incredibly vague problem next time I go over there?"

"They won't. Are either of you up for ice cream?"

"Not me," Jill said. "Jack will be home from work soon so I'm outta here. Later, Seth. Bye, Angel."

I waved to Jill as she hurried down the sidewalk and climbed into a white SUV.

"How about it?" Seth asked me.

"How about what?"

"Ice cream. Want to go to Fred's with me?"

"I'm new here, remember? I didn't even know Fred's had ice cream."

"Then I'll have to show you. Come on, I'll drive." Seth walked towards the street as though it was settled.

"I only brought my keys when I left the house," I said.

"Don't worry. I'll treat."

Chapter 11

I got into the passenger side of Seth's car. Most of the interior was light gray, but the floor mats were black. That was the only thing that stuck out to me more than the fact that I was in a car with a guy I'd just met. He asked my last name as we pulled away from the curb.

"Melling."

"Are you related to anyone in Hartford?"

"Not as far as I know."

"What brings you here then?"

"A job."

He nodded but did not ask what job.

"What's your last name?" I asked.

"Anderson."

"How often do you rescue people from your neighbors?"

Seth grinned. "I've done it a few times. Usually I just set a timer."

"That's funny," I said. I meant it to be sarcastic but I was laughing.

"So you've really never been to Fred's?"

"I've lived in Hartford less than two weeks."

"Oh, I know what we should do next then."

"Next? Do you plan on kidnapping me as long as Walt and Carol?"

"Yes," Seth said. "But it's okay because I'm more fun than they are." He winked at me as he parked in front of a restaurant with "Fred's Fine Food" in large yellow letters on the window. He jumped out first and I followed him again.

We were greeted by a young woman with short dark hair and a wary expression. "Hey, Seth. You know we're closing in five minutes." Someone else was putting chairs on tables at the back of the restaurant and there didn't appear to be any other customers.

I looked at my watch. How had it gotten to be 9 o'clock already?

Seth said, "Come on, Missy, we're just here for ice cream."

"You'll get brain freeze if you eat ice cream before we close."

Seth turned to me. "You like hot fudge sundaes, right?"

I nodded slowly, looking uncertainly at Missy.

He turned back to her and said, "Put it in those disposable cups you use for kids and we'll take it with us." He actually got down on his knees before he added, "Please."

She rolled her eyes at him. But she said, "Two hot fudge sundaes coming up."

"You'll love this. Missy makes the best sundaes." Seth appeared to be talking to me, but what he said was loud enough for Missy's benefit.

"You can probably get up now," I said.

"You're right. Help me." He held out his hand and I took it even though he clearly didn't need my help. He stood quickly and kept his hold on my hand, swinging our arms between us like we were a couple of six-year-olds.

"What are you doing?"

"I'm flirting with you. Is it working?" He smiled enough to show off some adorable dimples. If it hadn't been so obvious that he was kidding around, I might have been sucked in.

"Do *you* think it's working?" I asked.

He kept smiling and kept swinging my hand. "Oh, yeah," he said. "I know it's working because you're not letting go."

He sort of had a point. Maybe I was getting sucked in. He released my hand and waved to a group of younger guys walking past the window. They all waved back and stopped walking. Missy returned with two Styrofoam cups overloaded with whipped cream and two cherries each.

"Works of art," Seth told her as she handed him the cups. He passed them both to me and said, "Hold mine while I pay for them."

Missy pulled a pair of straws from a drawer under the register. "We don't have plastic spoons so you'll have to make do with these."

"No problem." Seth took the straws as he handed her some cash. "The change is for your excellent service." He made a slight bow and Missy was blushing furiously.

"Thanks," I said to her as we left. I was still holding both sundaes so Seth held the door for me.

There were four guys on the sidewalk. They all looked as though they were still in high school or only recently finished. One of them said, "Hey, Seth. We're headed to the park. You up for a game?" The guy next to him was holding a basketball so I guessed what kind of game they meant.

"Not tonight, guys. Angel here's never been to the old Hilson house."

"Oh," said the guy who had asked. A wave of understanding seemed to pass through the group and there were a few knowing smiles. I wondered what I had gotten myself into. Seth and the guys exchanged some farewells as the group moved on. He opened the car door for me and then took one of the cups. Once he was behind the driver's seat, he passed me a straw. Then he ate both cherries in a giant bite of whipped cream before he deposited his sundae in a cup holder.

"Where are we going?" I asked.

"The Hilson house. It's haunted."

"Where is that?"

"It's just outside of town." Seth had started the car. He made a U-turn and drove straight for what felt like about two miles. I was mostly trying to figure out how to eat ice cream with a straw and he was mostly laughing at me.

"Just poke the ice cream and then suck it out of the end."

That did work, but the bites were small and I just knew I'd be wearing some of it before I finished.

Seth pulled over to the side of the road in front of an old brick house. I had expected something rundown and spooky. This house was old, but it was well kept and even had two cars in the driveway and lights on downstairs.

"Is that it?" I asked.

"Yep." Seth turned off the car and then flashed his headlights twice. Another car parked a short distance ahead on the other side of the road also gave two flashes.

"What's the flashing all about?"

Seth said, "You're really not supposed to park out here so the double flash is a signal to other cars that we're just fellow ghost watchers and not the cops come to tell them to get lost. Or parents in the case of teenagers who might be out past curfew."

I nodded and looked back at the house. "Someone lives here?"

"Yeah… um, I forget her name. Something Hilson."

"It really doesn't look creepy at all. What makes people say this place is haunted?"

"Weird things happen every October."

"What kind of weird things?"

"Mostly lights and noises. I used to sneak around the back of the house with friends when I was younger. We'd lie in the grass and listen until we'd get scared off by unexplained thumps."

"But if people live here, doesn't that explain the noises?"

"Just wait," he insisted. "Something will happen."

"Something weirder than sitting in a car eating ice cream with straws while we wait for the police to come tell us to stop staring at someone's house?"

Seth wiggled his eyebrows at me. "Would you rather make out for a while?"

"I wouldn't want the ice cream to melt."

"Oh, so maybe later?"

I laughed at his teasing and tried to get another bite of my dessert. Missy did make a mean sundae.

"Look, they're coming outside." Seth nodded towards the house. It was on my side of the car. I saw a man and a woman come onto the porch. They walked around the house and appeared to go into a garage behind the house.

"Watch the upstairs window on the right," Seth said from behind me. A light turned on in that window a moment later and a shadow moved past the curtain. "Did you see that?"

"I did. But why am I supposed to think that wasn't just a person moving around up there?"

"Rebecca – that's her name – Rebecca is the only one who lives there and that's her car and her boyfriend's. We know they're in the garage. But mostly you think it's a person because you don't know the story." Seth nodded towards my window again and said, "Keep watching the house."

I turned and watched the fairly ordinary-looking house while Seth told me the story.

"There was a little girl who lived there at least fifty or sixty years ago now and she died. She was climbing a tree in the yard and she fell and hit her head on a rock."

"That's just sad," I said.

"That's not the creepy part. The same night she died, only a few hours later, there was a fire at a house down the street. I'll show you the foundation when we head back to town because that's all that's left. It completely burned down. Well, three kids were home alone at the time of the fire and they all swear that they got out only because the neighbor girl had come over to warn them. They hadn't heard yet that she died."

The story made my spine tingle. I realized only a second later that what I actually felt was Seth's fingertips brushing the back of my neck. I turned around to yell at him and nearly jumped out of my skin when I saw someone standing outside his window. Seth glanced over his shoulder and was still laughing as he rolled down his window to greet the police officer. "Hi, Jimmy," he said.

"Hey, Seth. You know I gotta tell you to move."

"Man, we just got here."

The officer, Jimmy apparently, leaned down to poke his head in the window. His voice was very deep so I was surprised to see that he looked younger than me. In fact, I wasn't sure he was old enough to be a police officer. "Did you see anything yet?" he asked.

"The light came on as soon as they went outside."

"No way."

Seth nodded seriously.

"No, really… I saw Rebecca today. She told me that she was tired of kids parking in front of the house to watch for the light so she took the bulb out."

"She took it out today?"

"Last night."

I looked back and saw that the upstairs was dark again. The house was beginning to look less ordinary.

Seth said, "By the way, this is Angel, um, Melling, right?"

"Yes," I said.

"Jimmy Larrick." He stuck his hand through the window and I shook it quickly. This was the guy who had caught the eye of Caitlin's sister. I didn't blame her. The uniform suited him. "Okay, guys," he said, "five minutes and then you gotta get out of here."

Seth saluted. "Yes, sir." He rolled up the window as Jimmy walked away and then shivered slightly. "When did it get cold?" he asked me.

"It's October and you're wearing shorts."

"I know what we can do to warm up." He grinned at me and I laughed only because I knew he was kidding.

But then he said, "We can dance."

"What?"

"Hang on… let me find a good song."

I wasn't sure what Seth had in mind. I didn't have much time to think about it because it only took him a few seconds to get a very upbeat song playing, loudly. He jumped out of the car and drummed his hands on the hood as he ran around to my side. He pulled the door open and reached in to grab both of my hands to pull me out.

I exited the car somewhat reluctantly. Not because he wanted me to dance in front of a house he'd been trying to convince me was haunted, but because I knew there were people there who might come out and ask what the heck we were doing. The music was almost as catchy as Seth's attitude though. I had a few minutes of fun dancing in the night. Then a slow song started. Seth pulled me close and pretended to look shocked. "Did you plan this?" he asked.

I laughed. "You picked the music."

"So I did." He dropped my hands. "We should go so we don't get Jimmy in trouble."

"Okay." I returned to the car and so did my driver.

He took me back to town, telling me random facts about the houses we passed on the way, and when we stopped in front of my house he said, "I hope you had fun."

"I did. And thanks for the ice cream."

"You're welcome. You didn't bring your phone with you, did you?"

I shook my head.

He handed me his. "Put your number in here and I'll text you mine in case you want to do this again." While I typed it in he said, "And you really should bring your phone when you visit Walt and Carol. Set an alarm before you get lured onto the porch and pretend it's an important call." He winked. "Works like a charm."

"I will keep that in mind. Goodnight, Seth." I got out and walked up to my house. I noticed that he waited until I got the door open so I turned and waved. He honked as he drove off.

By the time I checked my phone he had sent me a text that said:
Do you miss me yet?

Chapter 12

I had a review meeting with a parent during lunchtime on Friday so I couldn't eat with Caitlin. She stopped in to chat during an afternoon break though. Neither of us mentioned plans for dinner or the fact that she had tried to arrange something for me and Jon that night. She started by telling me about a kindergartner who had lost her first tooth during class. The poor girl had been so freaked out by the taste of blood that the teacher sent her to the office to call her mom. We were both a little torn between laughing and feeling sorry for the kid.

While we were trying not to laugh I got a text from Seth. It said: Why did the neighbor cross the road?

I put the phone down as soon as I read it because his joke could wait until after Caitlin left. But I asked her, "Do you know Seth Anderson?"

She had been standing in my doorway. At my question she practically threw herself into one of those short chairs in front of me. "Oh, no," she gasped. "Please don't tell me you like him."

"I only asked if you knew him. We just met last night."

"Of course I know Seth. The guy is a notorious heartbreaker. He goes around flashing those dimples and flirting with everyone, but he has the attention span of a gnat."

"So I shouldn't be doodling Angel Anderson on my files?"

Caitlin gave me a very serious look. "Tell me you are kidding."

"Of course I'm kidding. Do you really think I start imagining a wedding after an hour with a guy?"

Caitlin relaxed and smiled as though that was a ridiculous notion, which was great. That meant I hid it well. "Good," she said. "You are not allowed to fall for anyone else while I still have hopes of getting you together with my brother."

I hadn't forgotten about those hopes. Seth was a fun distraction, but I still felt as though Jon was a better match for me.

If I could get a chance to see him now that I knew he was available, perhaps I could convince him of that. And while I did want Caitlin's help if she could manage it, I did not want to be too obvious about it. I changed the subject. "How did you and Dan get together anyway?"

"He was one of Christopher's friends in high school. I had a big crush on him and he didn't pay any attention to me. Once he went away for school I kind of forgot about him. I moved back here after I finished college and didn't know that he was also back until about a year later. He called me out of the blue and wanted to get together to reminisce. I thought that was a little odd, but I agreed. Later he confessed that he'd recognized me at the town Fourth of July party and asked Chris for my number."

"Your brother didn't mind?"

"No, he knew Dan was a nice guy." Caitlin stood up with a sigh. "I better go. You have another kid soon, right?"

I checked the time. "Yeah."

Caitlin left and instead of pulling out a file right away I picked up my phone and replied to Seth: I give up. Why did the neighbor cross the road?

Seth: To rescue the pretty girl. Did it mean NOTHING to you?!

I smiled. He *was* a fun distraction. But I had work to do.

****

Two more parent meetings at the end of the day left me feeling ready for a weekend. I pulled on some yoga pants and a cozy fleece top and left my work clothes on the floor, something I never did. I flopped onto my couch and sighed. At some point I was going to have to feed myself. After a few minutes, I began to hear a strange clanking sound like metal scraping metal. I was more curious than I was weary so I moved across the room to peer out the window.

Riley Iverson was attacking some bushes in front of my house with hedge clippers and he was taking no prisoners. He finished all of them in the minute that I watched and hurriedly gathered the trimmings into a large paper bag. I assumed this was his latest excuse to visit me and I returned to my couch to wait for the doorbell. It didn't ring. Instead I heard a car start up and drive away. I looked outside again and Riley was definitely gone.

I still wasn't sure what to make of him anyway so I made my way to the kitchen to address dinner. I opened and closed my cupboards and my refrigerator several times before I gave up trying to convince myself to cook. Nothing easy sounded good. It felt like the ideal night to check out Pops.

I drove over there intending to get a small pizza to go. I hadn't reached the counter when a familiar voice called my name. Caitlin came running up to me. "This is perfect," she said with a wide grin. "Come join us."

I looked behind her and saw a man I knew was Dan. We hadn't officially met but I had seen him once or twice when he'd stopped by to visit Caitlin at the school. Sitting across from him in the booth was Jon. All I could think was that I was dressed for eating pizza in front of my TV. I was not dressed for trying to convince a guy that he might someday, in the not terribly distant future, want to recite some vows with me. My mouth went dry and I was sure I was going to trip over my feet as she practically dragged me to the red booth.

"Dan, this is my new friend Angel. I'm trying to talk her into joining us. That's okay with you guys, isn't it?"

I nodded a greeting to Dan as Caitlin introduced us and then nervously moved my eyes to Jon. Something was wrong. He looked tense, but I could tell he wasn't sharing my anxiety. He was angry. He removed himself from the booth, glaring at Caitlin as he did so. His voice had a forced calm as he said, "It is nice to see you again, Angel. I'm very sorry that my sister doesn't know how to mind her own business." He walked out.

Dan said, "What was that all about?"

Caitlin smacked herself on the forehead and said, "Oh, no! Oh, no!" She put her hand over her mouth for a second and then let it slide down. "He thinks I planned this. He thinks I tricked you into meeting us here."

"It does seem convenient," Dan remarked.

Caitlin shot him a dirty look. "I did *not* set this up."

He shrugged. "Sit down, Angel. You can still eat with the two of us. We'll sort things out with Jon later."

Caitlin slipped into the booth next to her husband and I took over Jon's seat. That felt less awkward than walking away. I wanted to go straight home to analyze what had just happened. I had thought for a second that I was about to sit down with Jon and

71

begin to figure out if my crush might lead somewhere nice, maybe towards an altar. But he didn't seem to want that chance. Was he upset with his sister because he thought she tricked him? Or was he worried about me getting the wrong idea from the set-up? Perhaps his earlier invitation had only been neighborly after all.

"I'm going to call Jon and get him back here," Caitlin said. She was already holding her phone.

"No, don't," I said. Dragging him back would not put either of us in the mood for a date.

Dan agreed with me. "You should explain later."

"But…" Caitlin stared at her phone. "I don't want him to be mad at me."

"You know Jon never stays mad. Even if you can't convince him you didn't set him up, he'll still get over it by tomorrow."

"One quick text," Caitlin said as she typed something on her phone. I wondered what she was telling him.

Dan looked at me. "We ordered a Hartford Special. Are you up for that?"

"Sure. I even know what that means."

"Look at you getting all assimilated," Caitlin said with a smile.

"So tell me," Dan said, "how often does my wife complain about me at work?"

"Not at all. She was a bit concerned about your interest in shag carpeting though."

"That would have been awesome."

"You mean aw*ful*," Caitlin said.

"Come on, it was cool."

Caitlin simply shook her head.

"Kitschy?" he suggested.

She continued to move her head side to side.

"So bad it was good?"

Caitlin sighed and said, "No."

"Fortunately for everyone," Dan said, "she loved my second choice."

"*Loved* might be a strong word for carpet, but I think we're both going to be happy with it."

The food arrived soon after that. Jon never came back. I didn't know if Caitlin had asked him to return. I enjoyed spending a little non-work time with her and meeting her husband. I felt guilty that the evening was still disappointing overall.

Chapter 13

My house was beginning to feel organized that Saturday morning. I'd been putting more effort into it since inviting George over to see the place. I didn't have a need for that small second bedroom so it had become the staging area for anything that didn't have an obvious home.

I was a little nervous about the evening. It wasn't the happy nervousness I felt when I thought about Jon. And that was the problem. I was thinking about Jon. I knew I couldn't pursue a relationship with George when Jon was taking over a lot of my brain as well as most of my hormones. But a terrible, awful, scared-of-being-alone-forever part of me didn't want to commit to being only friends with George before I knew for sure that Jon was not a possibility.

George was late. I didn't know him well. That still didn't seem like him. When he arrived, he was alone.

"You decided not to bring Mutt?" I asked, trying not to sound as though I had more interest in his dog.

"I couldn't... um, Mutt's gone."

"What do you mean gone?" I looked up and down the street behind George.

"I had some errands in the city this afternoon. When I came home Mutt was... he's dead."

I sucked in a huge gulp of air and held it until I realized I had nothing to do with it except let it back out. "What happened?"

"I don't know. I guess he wasn't really a young dog anymore though."

I didn't know what to say. If a dog I'd had for ten years died suddenly, I would not be able to function for a full day at least. George seemed subdued but not necessarily sad. I didn't want to dwell on the loss if that would make him feel worse. I said only,

"I'm sorry," and then stepped back to let him into the house. "Come in… I think I'm *almost* unpacked."

George looked around as he came inside. "I think I was here once a few neighbors ago. The place looks a bit different. More zebras." His eyes lingered on a painting of an entire herd of the black and white animal.

"I know," I said. "What can I say? Zebras are cool."

The sides of his mouth lifted slightly. I wasn't sure if he was agreeing with me or laughing at me. Mostly I was startled by the hint of happiness when I still thought I should be consoling him. I mean, I wanted to cry and I'd only spent a few hours with Mutt. I couldn't help that my mind was still on him. I asked George if he'd buried the dog.

"I'm going to do it tomorrow."

"Do you want company?"

"If you're offering, that would be nice."

"What time?"

"2 o'clock?"

"Okay. Um, what sort of errands did you have in Port… the city?"

"I stopped at a bookstore and I needed to pick up some heartworm medicine." He said it very matter-of-factly. His voice broke on the last word though. That's when I knew he was doing the guy thing. He was completely broken up and refusing to cry in front of me. I tried to respect that by suggesting we move into the kitchen.

"You can keep me company while I finish dinner."

"It smells good in here," he said. I think he was relieved to talk about food.

"Thanks." I turned on the oven light to get a peek at my quiche. "I hope you like it. There's also some chicken on the stove."

George leaned against the counter and nodded towards a cross-stitched zebra under a wall calendar. "Did you make that?"

"I did. That was one of my first zebras. I think I was sixteen or seventeen. A majority of the others have been gifts. Want to see the worst zebra anyone has ever given me?"

He nodded.

"Wait one second." I went into the extra bedroom alone – I didn't want him to see my mess – and dug through a few boxes as

74

quickly as I could. I found the statue and brought it back to the kitchen. It was resin and it was a zebra. It was also a lion with sharp teeth tearing into the zebra's hind leg. I held it up and George looked as appalled as I had been when I unwrapped it.

"Someone gave you a dying zebra?"

"It's hideous, isn't it?"

"Who gave that to you?"

"A guy I dated briefly in college."

"Did he really think you'd like that?"

I shrugged. "I'm not sure he put much thought into it. I think he just bought the first thing he found with a zebra on it."

George took the small statue and examined it more closely. "I suppose there's something to be said about the amount of detail but... well, I can be as clueless as the next guy and I still think it's pretty obvious this is not something you give to a girl who likes zebras."

"Yeah, it does sort of say 'dump me now.' I think I stuck with that guy only a few more weeks."

He handed the statue back to me. "If that's the worst zebra, what's the best? Do you have a favorite?"

"Hmm... that's a tough call." I stuck the ugly zebra on the counter rather than bother to hide it right away. "I guess I'd have to say the stuffed one on my bed because that's the only one I've named."

George smiled. "You know what I have to ask now, don't you?"

"You want to know what his name is?"

"Yes."

"Chocolate."

"Um..." He squeezed his eyebrows together. "Is it a brown zebra?"

"No. I named him a long time ago and I'm not sure what I was thinking but it stuck."

It looked as though dinner was nearly ready so I reached up and got two plates. George offered to put them on the table for me. I handed them over and grabbed glasses next. I studied him covertly while we set the table. He did have nice eyes, dark brown framed by darker lashes. If we found enough in common, would I be more excited to see them? Could a real love grow without the seed of infatuation?

We sat down to a calm dinner. We chatted about work and other mundane things. He complimented my cooking and had a second helping.

I think we noticed it at the same time, the small piece of chicken left on George's plate at the end of the meal. He had saved something for Mutt out of habit. He ate it bravely and swallowed hard. Then his elbow hit the table as he dropped his face onto his hand and his shoulders shook.

I ran to grab a box of tissues and felt the tears on my own face by the time I returned to the table. I dropped the box next to him and said, "Come here."

He took a tissue and then stood and let me hug him. I'm pretty sure I cried longer than he did but only because I wasn't trying to stop. It was a very sad moment. It was also oddly romantic. I was becoming aware of how nice it felt to have a man's arms around me. It had been a long time. He picked his head up to look at me and didn't let go. I knew he was about to kiss me. He moved so slowly I expected something soft and testing. His mouth covered mine with a clear hunger and I let myself enjoy the salty taste for a few seconds even though it felt wrong. It felt as though he was searching me for comfort, not love.

I broke away.

George said, "I'm sorry."

"No, it's okay. I just…"

"No, that was… I should go."

I didn't protest and began to walk him out.

"Thanks for dinner," he said as we reached the door.

"I'll still be over tomorrow."

He nodded and stepped outside.

I closed the door with a sense of disappointment. I felt lonelier than ever. But two lonely people did not necessarily belong together. George seemed to know that, too.

I cleared the table after he left. I did not bother to wash the dishes. I washed my face with warm water and sat down to try to find something on TV that would make me laugh. My phone interrupted with a new text a few minutes later. Seth had sent: Here's a riddle. I am outside your house and you did not expect me. I am not a stalker. Who am I?

76

I got up and looked out my front window. There were a few cars parked on the street and I thought one of them might be Seth's. I typed: `Are you really outside my house?`

Seth: `Answer the riddle.`

Me: `Seth?`

Seth: `You're close.  The answer is a surprise date.  Are you free?`

Me: `Right now?`

Seth: `Spontaneity is my middle name.  Are you coming out or am I going in?`

I checked my reflection. I did not look as though I had recently been crying. It was Saturday night. Jon might have been upset because he wasn't interested in me. Seth was single and had cute dimples. I sent: `Give me five minutes.`

I went into my bedroom and picked out a bright blue cardigan. I stuffed my phone into my purse. Without knowing what Seth had in mind I didn't know how else to prepare. I opened my front door and found Seth standing on the other side.

His light gray dress shirt was wrinkled around the waist as though it had been tucked in earlier in the day. He had his hands behind his back and he grinned at my surprised expression. "It's like you didn't know I was here or something."

"I thought you were in your car," I said.

"Maybe I was and maybe I wasn't." He smiled mischievously and produced a pair of daisies from behind his back. "These are for you."

"Aw, thank you." I took the flowers and brought them to my nose.

"I knew I had to step up my game because I saw what's-his-name from over there at your house. And there's nothing weird about that because I just happened to be coming home from work when I saw him leaving."

Now I understood. Seth wasn't at my door because he missed me – as some of his persistent texts had claimed – but because his sense of competition had been sparked. "Yeah," I said, "it's only a little weird that you know he was here. So what are we doing tonight?"

Seth gasped and put his hand over his heart. "Are you suggesting that I ruin the surprise?"

I didn't want to laugh. The last thing he needed was encouragement. I turned away to leave the flowers in the house before I locked my front door. The best I could do was attempt to cover my amusement with activity.

He took my hand to lead me to his car. As he opened the door for me he said, "No peeking in the backseat," which of course made me want to look in the backseat. I took a very quick glance as he ran around to his side.

He started up the car and said, "You peeked, didn't you?"

"I couldn't help it," I confessed. "It's all covered with blankets anyway."

"Are you sure about that?"

"Are you trying to make me look again?"

Seth flashed those dimples at me. "Are you trying to blame me for your own weakness?"

"Will you tell me where we're going?"

He appeared to consider the question. "You'll know in a minute anyway. We're going to the park."

I thought about trying to get another hint, but since we were staying in Hartford it wouldn't be long before I saw for myself what Seth was up to. I very patiently tapped my fingers against the armrest.

Hartford had a decent-sized town park. There was a bunch of playground equipment on one end near a patch of blacktop painted for basketball and tennis, though obviously both games could not be played at the same time. Two baseball diamonds were at the far end where Seth parked. He got out and began rummaging under a blanket in his backseat. By the time I had walked around the car, he had pulled out a blue kite. He tore off the packaging and threw that into the backseat.

"What do you intend to do with that?" I asked.

"It's a kite," he said.

"I know."

"What do people normally do with kites?"

"But it's dark," I said.

Seth put on a very serious expression as he tucked the kite under one arm. Then he held his hands up as though he was holding an imaginary beach ball and said, "The earth is round you see, and when it turns away from the sun…"

I gently slapped his hand. "I know *why* it's dark. I mean, if you fly a kite in the dark, you won't be able to see it."

"Oh, ye of little faith."

"What does that mean?"

He grinned and motioned for me to follow him. "Come on."

We walked onto the closer ball field and stopped at the pitcher's mound. There were a couple of lights in the parking lot so it wasn't completely dark. It still didn't feel as though flying a kite at night was a great idea, despite the substantial wind blowing my hair across my face. Seth unfolded the kite and slipped in the plastic supports. "Bennet Real Estate" was printed across it in red and white letters.

"Where did you get that?" I asked.

"Snagged it from work."

"You're a real estate agent?"

He nodded and handed the kite to me. The job fit. Seth was clearly born to sell things. "Wait here," he said.

I stood and watched him jog towards a small white shed beyond the field, somewhere past third base. I couldn't tell if he went inside it or behind it. A few seconds later there was a loud clicking sound and the field was flooded with light. I wondered if anyone could switch on the field lights or if that was one of his superpowers. He returned to my side looking as satisfied as if he had actually turned the earth back towards the sun.

With the wind's help, it only took us a few attempts to get the kite off the ground. Seth was holding the plastic spool and occasionally letting the kite go higher. "Now we start guessing how we'll lose the kite," he said.

"You plan to lose it?"

He shrugged. "I have never successfully brought home a kite after flying it. If it gets off the ground, it will invariably get tangled in something or the string will break. Which do you think?"

"The wind is pretty strong. I suppose the string *could* break."

He held it out to me. "You should have a turn before it gets away."

"I'm happy to watch."

"I insist."

I took the spool and rewrapped a bit of loose string.

"It looks as though you've done this before," he said, "which makes it even more obvious when I help." He stood behind me and put his right hand over mine and reached around to grab the string with his left. My heart sped up and my neck tingled as he leaned in to my ear and whispered, "Isn't this better than watching?"

It *was* better. And it was so so so so so much worse. I was starting to like him. Seth was a fun while it lasted kind of guy, not a happily ever after kind of guy. Falling for him would only delay what I knew I wanted. I tried to relax and focus on the kite in front of me and not the guy behind me. This was nothing more or less than an evening with a new friend. I felt a tug of wind on the kite and let out more string, the last of it, and it wasn't well secured to the spool.

The kite snapped away from us. I watched it float higher for a moment and when I turned around Seth had the side of his finger in his mouth. "You okay?" I asked.

"Just a bit of rope burn when it slipped away. Who knew kites were dangerous?"

"*You* knew it was going to get away."

"Do I get a prize for being right about that?" He winked at me as he sucked on his finger again. The action drew way too much attention to his mouth. I simply shook my head. He grinned broadly as though he knew exactly what I had just been thinking. He said, "Are you hungry?"

"Not particularly."

"I haven't had any kind of dinner yet. Would you snack a bit if I ate?"

"Do you have food?"

"Of course. I'm like a Boy Scout only… well, older and no neckerchief."

"Okay. Let's eat then."

"I gotta turn the lights off. Meet me back at the car." He jogged towards that white shed again. We had ended up closer to first base so I walked slowly back to his car. The lights shut off just before I got there.

I was still holding a white piece of plastic that used to have kite string around it. I tossed it into a nearby trash can while I wondered what else Seth had in his backseat. I leaned over and pressed my hands to the window in a blatant attempt to find out. But only after he was close enough to see me do it.

He didn't say anything but he flashed those dimples again when he saw me. I stood back to watch as he pulled a large folded blanket out of the backseat and proceeded to drape it across the hood of his car. He pulled out two smaller blankets next. The blue one he handed to me and the green one he threw over his shoulder. I had no idea what to do with the one I was now holding. Seth leaned into the back of his car and came out holding a plastic shopping bag from the Market. "Come on," he said as he closed the door.

I was only confused as to where we were headed for a few seconds. He patted the blanket on the hood and said, "You take this side," before he walked around the front of the car and jumped onto the other side of the hood.

"You want me to sit on your car?" I asked.

"Sure. You need help?" He held out his hand to me.

I shook my head and climbed up next to him. He placed the bag between us and opened it. "What do you feel like?"

I checked the bag's contents. It had an assortment of small bags of chips and tiny candy bars as well as a couple of sandwiches. I said, "Chocolate," as I helped myself to something that looked tasty.

Seth took out a sandwich, but he dropped it again as he said, "I forgot something."

I crossed my legs and arranged the blue blanket over my lap as Seth disappeared into the back of his car again. He handed me a bottle of water as he returned. Then he pulled a small battery-powered candle from behind his back and set it between us. "I figured real fire could be bad on this sloped surface, but you get the idea."

"What idea?" I asked seriously, doubting if he could be serious for one question. He seemed to be going through a lot of trouble to show me a good time if that's all it was.

He wiggled his eyebrows at me and said, "You know, ambiance."

No more wishful thinking for me. I popped a piece of chocolate into my mouth while Seth opened his sandwich. A rush of wind drew my attention to a line of trees along the edge of the parking lot. Some of the leaves were still green and others were red and orange and yellow. The wind forced a shower of them to the ground.

Seth began to describe the history of the park during his lifetime. He pointed out which playground structures were the

81

oldest and why the random platform on springs had once made sense. I kept my head the whole time and was pleased with the fact that I was still thinking of him as a friend when he took me home. But he didn't just drop me off. He walked up to my house and stood on the porch while I unlocked my door. "Thanks for the interesting night," I said. "It was fun."

"Fun enough that I get a goodnight kiss?" He looked at me with hopeful eyes and a hint of dimples. I had to summon more of my resolve not to fall for him.

"Maybe next time," I said.

He grinned. "I can settle for the promise of a next time."

He was about to step off the porch when I thought better of my answer. Even if Seth was not capable of being serious, I was. "Seth, wait."

He turned to face me.

"I need to say that… well, I'm not interested in messing around. I'm glad we're friends but you shouldn't flirt with me if you're not trying to start a real relationship."

I couldn't read his reaction. He simply stared at me before he smiled and said, "I will take that under advisement. Goodnight, Angel." He waved over his shoulder as he skipped down the steps.

I went into my house and prepared for bed. Soon I noticed that Seth had already texted me. His message said: That was a promise, right?

Did he even know when he was doing it?

Chapter 14

I let myself linger in bed Sunday morning because I was going to the evening Mass with Ashley and Jeff. I had planned that when I was trying to avoid Jonathon Thorpe. I figured it still wouldn't hurt to examine the evening regulars. Perhaps one of them would be a guy my age who affected me like Jon, who pursued me like Seth, and who was dying to start having kids. And maybe he had a good job and a nice family and a big house in Hartford right next to the park. I had been picturing pushing my future kids on those swings.

I hugged Chocolate the zebra because he was all I had after I quit the fantasy.

By the time I showered and dressed, it was nearly 11 am. I didn't know if I should call the peanut butter and jelly sandwich I ate then breakfast or brunch or lunch. The only thing that seemed to matter was that no one was there to hear me call it the wrong name.

I still had a few hours before the dog burial and it occurred to me that I should bring something. Maybe some flowers for the grave or... I suppose what I really wanted was something I could present in Mutt's memory that would somehow make the awkward kiss less awkward. There was little chance of finding anything like that but I found myself wandering down Main Street around noon anyway. That was when I thought something might be open on a Sunday.

I planned to end at the Market and use its skimpy pet section as a last resort. I passed a bar and a place for haircuts, both closed. I saw a bank and an insurance company, both also closed and not exactly places to buy gifts anyway. There was a small store called "Things to Do" and I crossed the street to get a better look. It was closed on Sundays. I peered through the window for future reference and saw that it was a craft or hobby store. I walked on and the next building was empty. I didn't see what was after that before I heard someone calling my name.

I turned around to face a woman with jet black hair tied up in short pigtails with pink bows. She was familiar but I didn't immediately remember how I knew her.

"It is Angel, right?" she asked as I got closer.

"Yeah, um, Jill?"

"That's right. I'm Seth's sister."

"How are you?"

"Good. I saw you peeking in the window of my store and wondered if you needed something."

"'Things to Do' is yours?"

She nodded proudly. "Best job ever."

"I'll have to check it out sometime when you're open."

"Come on in now," Jill said as she motioned me towards the door.

"I don't want to bother you."

"It's not. I just said it was the best job. And you look like you need something." She opened the door and nodded for me to go in ahead of her. I was curious and fairly desperate for an idea so I went inside. Jill flipped on another light and turned to face me. "What do you need?" she asked.

I needed a husband. That was a problem for a different day. "Well, my neighbor's dog died and I wanted to get something to..."

"Wait a minute! You don't mean George Baumgartner, do you?"

I nodded.

"Not Mutt! Oh, he was the sweetest thing." She held a hand to her cheek.

"I know. I'm going over there to help bury him and I thought something for the grave might be nice."

Jill nodded solemnly. "I am so glad I let you in. Let's see what we can find." She stood still and stared at the ceiling. I wondered if perhaps she had her inventory memorized. Since I didn't have that advantage, I began to scan the nearby shelves.

She had a little bit of everything. Yarn and knitting needles and paint by number kits and beads and decks of cards. Everything looked rather happy though. Nothing felt appropriate to express sorrow.

Apparently, Jill had better luck. She snapped her fingers and said, "I've got it." She walked away and I followed her to the other side of her store. She picked up a small box and held it up for me to see. It was a mosaic stone kit. "It's kind of intended for kids to write their names. You spell Mutt and it might be a nice marker."

I took the box for a closer look. It had blue stones for spelling a name and multicolored stones to surround it. The finished product was only six inches. It felt like a reasonable offer and I could probably find someone to give it to if George didn't want it. "Okay," I said, "I'll get this."

Something else caught my eye as I approached the register. Hanging below the counter was a craft kit that appeared very old. The instructions and the plastic bag were slightly yellowed. The kit created an odd-looking wreath and it caught my eye because of something black and white. I picked up the package before I realized it was a cat. The wreath was still sort of cool because it was unusual. It had brown and silver wire something like artificial grapevine and tiny glass flowers.

Jill let me study the picture for a few moments before she said, "It just needs a zebra, right?"

"How do you know I like zebras?"

"You've been in town long enough for a few basic facts to surface. And I have a zebra." She reached behind her to a shelf of small rubbery animals and pulled out a zebra. It was just the right size to replace the cat on the wreath. It would still be a weird decoration, but it would be my kind of weird.

"All right. I'll buy the stone and the wreath and the zebra. I'm glad you let me in, too."

Jill smiled. "A friend of mine found that wreath for me. I suspect it's going to make this zebra extra special. Maybe it will even be your last one."

"Why would it be my last zebra?"

"Some collections are eventually complete."

I didn't know if the strange silver wreath would complete my zebra collection but I knew I wanted it to be part of it. I paid for everything and thanked Jill. She asked me to share her condolences with George as well.

I brought the mosaic with me unopened when I went to his house. I was walking up the sidewalk when I heard the sound of a shovel from the backyard. I let myself in through a wooden gate next to the house.

"You started without me?" I said as I took in George standing over a hole in the ground. Judging by the blanket-wrapped shape that was drawing my attention and forcing me to look away, the hole was nearly large enough.

George stopped and rested the shovel on the ground next to him. "I thought I'd get the hole dug before you got here," he said. "I only have one shovel anyway."

"I'm here for whatever you want me to do, even if that means standing around feeling useless."

He nodded slightly and then scooped out several more loads of dirt without either of us saying anything. There was a clicking sound whenever the blade nicked a rock and I was still not thinking about what was in the blanket. George forced the shovel into the ground next to the hole so that it stood straight up on its own. He sighed and brushed his hands together. "That's probably deep enough."

"I think so," I said. I fiddled with the box in my hands. "Do you know Jill, um, I guess her last name used to be Anderson?"

"From the craft store?"

"Yes, that Jill. I ran into her today and we thought this might work, you know, as a grave marker." I showed him the box in my hand. "If we write Mutt on it. Is that a bad idea?"

"No, I hadn't thought about... I like this. Thanks." He took the box and opened it to see inside. "We'll need water and... Let's do this inside before we... finish."

I followed him through the back door and we focused on the instructions for the project. He mixed the compound and asked me to arrange the stones. I did my best with my limited artistic ability and kept asking his opinion. The project did make things less awkward, but it still felt as though there was something unresolved between us. I felt him look away quickly a few times and knew I was doing the same.

We left the finished mosaic to dry as we returned to the backyard. George stood between the hole and the blanket looking hesitant. We both knew what came next and I wasn't sure I could do it if he asked me.

He eventually knelt next to the blanket and carefully lifted it. A small brown paw slipped out of a fold in the bottom and caused my eyes to burn. I dabbed at them with a tissue. George crouched next to the waiting grave and deposited the bundle as gently as if he were trying not to wake a sleeping newborn. My heart ached for what I was watching and for what I would never see.

He picked up the shovel again and simply held it for a minute. Then he made a move to scoop some dirt but turned the shovel over before he picked anything up. It rested on the loose dirt while I tried to figure out how to offer to do what I didn't want to do. I took a tentative step forward. George suddenly thrust the shovel in my direction and said, "Can you...?"

I took it quietly and tried not to notice George wiping the back of his hand across his eyes. He had done the hardest part. I began to refill the hole with loose dirt. I tipped the first few shovelfuls as carefully as I could. Once the blanket was covered with dirt, George took the shovel back and filled the rest of the hole quickly. He tapped it down and exhaled slowly.

I'm not sure how long we both stared at the fresh grave. Minutes ticked by and I began to wonder if my presence was still helpful or if it had been helpful at all. George turned to me and said, "I appreciate you coming over." At first I thought that was my cue to leave. He continued though, "I would have felt weird asking one of my guy friends to... I mean... well, thanks."

I nodded, thinking maybe now I should leave.

George said, "About yesterday..."

"We don't have to talk about that now."

"I just want to say I'm sorry again."

"You didn't really do anything wrong."

"I think... you clearly didn't want me to..."

"I did actually. I mean, I did right then. But I just don't think..." I sighed. I knew what I wanted to say and I was only making things worse by stretching it out. "I liked the kiss but I don't think I see a future for us so we probably shouldn't do it again."

George gave a small smile and I couldn't tell whether or not it was forced. "I think you're right so please don't feel bad about being honest. You should know that I'll still be right across the street if you ever need anything."

"Same here."

I exited through the same gate I had entered feeling sad about Mutt and sad about ending what wasn't a relationship anyway. But still proud of the grownup resolution. It was so much better than the way I handled things with Parker. I was still occasionally waving at him and pretending we hadn't had a horrible date.

Chapter 15

I drove to Jeff and Ashley's house late in the afternoon. They were going to feed me dinner before we went to church. Jeff disappeared into the kitchen to cook and to avoid the conversation Ashley couldn't wait to begin.

"Has the novelty of the new girl worn off or are you still Hartford's most eligible bachelorette?" she asked me almost as soon as we were seated in a familiar living room.

"I think you're exaggerating."

"Come on, didn't you have two dates last weekend?"

I smiled. Maybe she wasn't exaggerating. "I actually had two dates last night."

"Really?! At the same time?"

"No. You know George was coming over, right? Well, he left early and Seth surprised me with a trip to the park."

"Seth is the guy you just met on Thursday?"

"Yeah."

"And he was over again on Saturday? I'm not sure about that guy."

"I haven't figured out how harmless he is. It's possible he's on some sort of conquest and he might just like to flirt. Either way, I think one of us will get bored before anyone gets hurt."

"Are you sure about that because you don't sound bored when you talk about him."

Ashley knew me too well. "All right. I admit I like him a little bit. But I know he has no real intentions and... I'll be okay."

"So that's Parker and George and Seth..." Ashley began to count the guys on her fingers. "And Riley?"

"I don't know if he gave up or... well, I never knew if he was making excuses to stop by – which would have been kind of sweet – or if he was too dense to know his dad was making up excuses to send him."

89

"Hmm, four guys and none of them with any hope for a real relationship. That's disappointing."

"Thank you for spelling out all my failures."

"It's not a failure to be incompatible with someone."

"I know. It still feels like it."

"Maybe you should call Riley."

"I don't know. I'd hate to…I'd feel worse if I had to tell him it wouldn't work out if I had been the one to try to start something."

Jeff leaned around the corner from the kitchen. "I have to speak for the guys here. Why do you think it'd be any easier to get rejected after going out on a limb?"

"Because if he asks and it doesn't work it's like saying, 'No, thank you,' but if I ask and it doesn't work it's like saying, 'Oh, sorry… I thought you'd be a much better catch.'"

Jeff stared at me for a moment and then turned to Ashley. "I'm sorry, honey, but that is the dumbest thing your sister has ever said."

"You haven't known her as long as I have," she retorted.

I gave her a gentle shove but didn't really try to defend myself. All three of us knew I was making up a desperate excuse for being afraid of rejection myself. And one of us knew I was also trying not to admit my other reason for not pursuing Riley. His name was Jon.

Jeff faded back into the kitchen and Ashley said, "Have you reconsidered signing up for-"

"No." I cut her off because I knew what she was going to say. She had been suggesting I try online dating since she'd met Jeff that way. "I don't want to move again and I think the odds of finding someone from Hartford, or even Port Harris, are not good."

"You're probably right about that and I don't want you to move either." Ashley unbuttoned the top button on her jeans while she talked. She'd been complaining that her clothes were getting tight. She still didn't look any rounder to me. "Hey!" she said. "What about Jon? I can't believe you thought he was married when he wasn't. Have you seen him since you found out?"

"I did see him and it was kind of bad."

"How bad?" Ashley leaned forward with curiosity.

"I went to get pizza like I said I was going to and he was there. He was with Caitlin and her husband and she invited me to join them and Jon thought she set it up."

"Set it up how?"

"Apparently, he thought she asked me to meet her at Pops without saying the guys would be there. He felt tricked and he got mad and left."

"Oh, no. He wasn't mad at you though, was he?"

I shook my head. "No. He thought I was tricked, too. It was still disappointing. I have a plan though."

"You have a plan?" Ashley smirked.

"I do. It's totally pathetic but I'm going to stake out the Market."

"What?"

"Well, I bumped into him there the last two Mondays. So I'm going to watch for him tomorrow and bump into him on purpose. I figure I can start by apologizing for the confusion on Friday and just see if we can get a conversation going."

Ashley grinned suggestively. "And then you ask him out?"

"What? No! Then I get him to ask me out."

Jeff poked his head around the corner again and said, "Give the guy a break. You already turned him down. It's your turn to make a move."

"Tracking him down at the Market *is* my move."

"He's not going to know that. Isn't the whole point to make it look like you just happened to run into him?"

"Yes, but once we start talking I'm sure there will be enough sparks for him to get the idea."

Jeff rolled his eyes and went back into the kitchen.

"I thought you didn't want anything to do with this conversation," I called to him. He did not respond. He probably thought it best not to say too much about my cowardice. I knew he asked Ashley out in an email.

I turned back to my sister. "Did you get the ultrasound scheduled?"

"Yep. Only two more weeks until we find out if it's a boy or a girl."

"And if it's a girl, you're going to name her Angel, right?"

"Don't you think that would be confusing?" she said instead of laughing. I could tell she wanted to laugh but I didn't mind because I was joking.

"We already decided on Bathsheba," Jeff called from the kitchen.

Ashley snorted. "I think he feels left out. You want to move into the kitchen to talk?"

"All right." I followed her to the next room and the sight of food being prepared naturally changed the subject. That was fortunate because I didn't want to talk about the baby anymore.

I didn't meet any new people at church that night. Unless you count the four-year-old girl who walked up to me and told me her name before she lifted up her dress to show me how many layers it had.

****

Work was pretty normal on Monday except that Caitlin called in sick. I wasn't sure if that was good or bad. I mean, of course I felt bad that she was sick. But I wanted to ask her if she'd smoothed things over with Jon before I talked to him. On the other hand, asking if he knew how she was feeling would give me something else to say.

I had an audio book playing in my car while I waited in the parking lot. This served two important purposes. The first was obviously to alleviate the boredom of waiting in a parking lot. The second was a plausible excuse if Jon somehow noticed that I was sitting in my car when he arrived and still came inside after him. I could say that I wanted to finish a chapter before I got out of the car.

I finished several chapters and I still didn't see him. When it was at least a half hour past when I had seen him the last two times, I gave up and drove home without buying any food. A scary and somewhat irritating voice in my head suggested that he didn't show up because he was avoiding me. I think I managed to convince that voice that Jon just wasn't as predictable as I was. I planned to try again on Tuesday. He would need food eventually and there was only one grocery store in Hartford.

I spent the remainder of my evening putting together the wreath I'd bought on Sunday and answering texts from Seth about when we were going to get together again. He wasn't suggesting an actual time or place, but teasing me with ridiculous ideas. One of them involved getting arrested and having to share a cell. Another asked how tall a ladder he'd need to get to my bedroom window so we could elope. I reminded him that I lived alone in a one-story house. He replied that there was nothing romantic about ringing the doorbell.

Caitlin was back at work on Tuesday. She was carrying tissues with her everywhere she went and insisted on coming no closer than my doorway when she stopped to tell me exactly what I wanted to hear. "I explained the coincidence to Jon," she said.

I nodded. "So he's not upset with you anymore?"

"He tried to be difficult about it by saying that it was still my fault because if I hadn't been trying so hard to fix you two up in the first place then he wouldn't have assumed I was still trying. Anyway, he's fine. But I still don't know how I'm going to get you guys together if he won't cooperate."

I tried a little fishing. "Do you think he'd be more receptive if you tried to fix him up with someone else?"

"Oh, no! Don't tell me you're backing out on me, too?"

She misunderstood. "No, I'll cooperate if you want me to. I just thought maybe I was the reason Jon isn't interested."

Caitlin eyed me funny for a minute. She didn't tell me what I wanted to hear. She said, "You just cooperate. It'll be fine." She smiled as she covered her face with a tissue and walked down the hall.

Chapter 16

I had decided there were three equal possibilities for Jon's reluctance. He didn't want Caitlin to fix us up because he thought *I* wasn't interested because of that whole turning him down thing. He didn't want her to fix us up because *he* wasn't interested and had only meant to be friendly before. Or he simply didn't want his sister involved in his love life.

It might have even been all three. I felt that I could only investigate by talking to him myself. That was why I was listening to the same audio book in the same parking space at the Hartford Market after work on Tuesday. If Jon didn't show up I might have to go inside for a few things, at least to tide me over until Wednesday.

After a while, a familiar car pulled into the lot a safe distance from me. I sank a little lower in my seat. It was Jon. He got out and stuffed his keys in his pocket. He glanced around the parking lot and I held my breath until he started walking toward the store. His jacket was unzipped and I could see his work shirt under it. Maybe it was the idea of a steady job or maybe it was a good color on him, but there was something very attractive about that shirt. I liked the buttons even though I had to make my mind stop thinking about undoing those buttons.

The blast of cool air felt nice as I opened my car door. I walked through the old door of the Market. It made a whooshing noise as it closed behind me and I placed my hands on a shopping cart handle. My plan was to start shopping normally. If I didn't naturally run into Jon after a few aisles, I would accelerate the search. I placed a few fruits and vegetables in my cart and started down the first aisle. I saw Jon turning at the end of it. New plan. I swung my cart around so that I would go down the same aisle facing him.

There was one other shopper between us and Jon noticed me as soon as the old man passed him. I smiled. Jon did the same. He put his hand on the back of his neck for a moment and plucked something off the shelf next to him. I parked my cart just before we reached each other. "Hi, Jon," I said.

"Hi, Angel. I guess I was really on to something when I said we'd be bumping into each other in town."

"Yes. And you know that's what happened on Friday, right? Just a coincidence?"

He nodded. "Yeah, I should apologize for being rude that night."

"No, don't worry. I understand why you thought what you did. Caitlin's been…"

"She's bugging you, too? *That* I'm sorry about." He appeared embarrassed at his sister's behavior.

"I think she means well."

He shrugged and didn't say anything.

My brain froze. I could not waste this opportunity.

Jon said, "Well, I guess I better let you shop." He began moving again.

I said only, "See you later," and numbly pushed my cart forward.

I was still kicking myself horribly for not making better use of "accidentally" running into Jon as I rounded the corner with my shopping cart and realized what was about to happen. Jon and I were going to pass each other in the next aisle as well. Even from the other end I could tell he was biting back a smile. I pulled a few cans off the shelf because in addition to wanting this to look like a casual shopping trip, I did need food.

"Hello again," he said as he got closer.

At that point my brain unfroze and I had a brilliant idea. I turned my cart the same direction as his. "It'd be silly to keep passing each other. I'll just walk with you."

"Okay," he said. His tone was perfectly relaxed. I needed to get a conversation going in order to appear just as calm about it.

"I, um, I think I'm pretty much unpacked now. I just have a few boxes of things I can't quite decide where to put them."

"Yeah? And you're finding your way around all right?"

"I haven't gotten lost once."

"You say that as though it's possible to get lost in Hartford. We have like four streets."

I laughed at his exaggeration. "Hartford is not that small. You could get lost here for a minute."

"Maybe." He shrugged at me. "I've never tried."

"Which of the four streets do you live on, by the way?"

His face tensed somewhat as though he was fighting a smile. "I don't think I should tell you that."

"What are you afraid of?"

"Nothing. I just like to keep a certain level of mystery."

"Hmm… I bet Caitlin would tell me."

"I don't think you want to ask her. She'd read something into it."

He looked as though that would be bad. But would it be bad for Caitlin to think I was interested because he thought I didn't want that or because he didn't want that? I thought Jon had a little too much mystery going for him as I picked up a box of spaghetti noodles.

"Can you hand me one of those, please?" he asked.

"Sure." I picked up another box and passed it to Jon. I held on a second too long. Could he tell how nervous he made me?

"So I think you've been making friends with some of your neighbors already."

It wasn't a question, but he said it like it was a question. That was good because it gave me something to talk about. "I met Seth Anderson from down the street a few days ago and he took me to some house outside of town and tried to convince me it was haunted."

"Oh, the old Hilson house."

"So you're familiar with it?"

"Yes, but I haven't actually sat out there since I was in high school."

"And what did you think? Is it haunted?"

"I doubt it." He seemed to consider the matter before he elaborated. "I definitely saw some weird stuff. I was usually convinced that the old woman who lived there was just playing tricks, but there was something about that house that made it hard to be sure."

"It did look a little creepy. Maybe I need to see it again though with someone who isn't telling me ghost stories." *Like you*, I thought. He should volunteer to take me now.

He said, "I remember one of the first times I was there. We heard this loud scraping noise and saw what looked like a person falling off the roof and then Ms. Hilson came out with a flashlight like she had heard it, too. And she looked all over the yard and didn't find anything. It was spooky. She might have been playing with us, but it was dark and it was two nights before Halloween so we couldn't help being a little scared."

"Maybe I don't need to see the house again. I don't think I'd have let Seth take me out there if I thought I was actually going to see something scary."

"Not a fan of scary movies then?"

I shook my head firmly. "Or scary books or... I think I'd be perfectly happy if everyone dressed up as cartoon characters for Halloween."

Jon smiled. "I think Ethan wants to be a fireman this year. That's not too scary."

"He'll be adorable. Do you think I'd get a lot of trick-or-treaters where I live?"

"Yeah. You'll want lots of candy if you turn your light on."

I nodded. I could handle scary costumes on people half my size. "If I carved a pumpkin, would it get smashed?"

"Probably not. People seem to be pretty good about that but I'm not making any promises. We do have a contest though."

"For pumpkin carving?"

"Yeah, there are three face categories. Scary faces – your favorite – silly faces and... I don't remember the other one. And then there's a category for other stuff. Emma won a few years ago with a cat. It was really good but don't tell anyone I said that."

I was staring at a wall of cereal and too distracted to decide what kind I wanted. Jon grabbed a box quickly and then seemed to be waiting for me. That was a good sign. I started moving again and said, "How long have you worked with your dad?"

"Feels like forever. He and his best friend bought the garage," he tapped the logo on his shirt, "from a guy who was retiring when I was a kid. I think I was eight or nine and it was only a few years later that I started going out there on Saturdays to watch. I sort of gradually became an employee as I learned more."

"Is it weird to have your dad as a boss?"

"Usually it's great. He likes to kid around a lot though."

"I got that impression."

Jon smiled and quickly squelched it. Something inside me sort of melted a little. "Dad's favorite thing," he said, "is to come out while I'm working and pretend to freak out over something I've done wrong. Sometimes he does it in front of customers. This one time it was this guy who didn't know Dad likes to joke – he wasn't from Hartford – and the guy totally thought I was destroying his car. It was bad." Jon gave me a sideways look. "Why are you laughing? I just said it was bad."

"I'm sorry. That's funny."

"You're not sorry," he said through his own laugh. "But it is funny... now. It wasn't so funny at the time. The guy was livid."

"Is your dad a little more careful about when he does that sort of thing?"

"I think so. It's still funnier when he does it to Tommy." Jon flicked something off a shelf into his cart. "You know Tommy's my brother, right? Ethan's dad."

I nodded. I knew exactly who Tommy was *now*. Maybe this was an opening to explain my mistake. I was trying to figure out if I could explain what I had thought without bringing up the dinner invitation because I didn't want to be caught making the wrong assumption again. I had time to think while we split up to let another shopper pass us. I lost my train of thought when I noticed a line of plastic bag clips hanging from a shelf. They were animal shapes. Jon saw me looking through them and asked, "Are you looking for a zebra?"

I nodded. There were no zebras though. Jon unhooked a monkey. "You need this one," he said.

"That's a monkey."

"Yes, it is."

"I don't collect monkeys."

"That's why you should get this. It'll give your zebras something to talk about."

"What are *you* talking about?"

"It's common knowledge. Zebras like to talk about monkeys."

I laughed harder than I should have. There was something funny about the way he said it as though he wasn't trying to be funny. Another shopper needed to get past us. I collected my composure as Jon caught up to me again. I noticed that the monkey clip was in his cart. Neither of us mentioned that. "What made you want to be a speech therapist?" he asked.

"Oh, um, my aunt was one. I could tell she enjoyed it and she... well, I saw that she was able to do it part time. She scheduled clients only while her kids were in school and it seemed like a good balance. You know, staying home with her kids, but still having a little something for herself."

Jon appeared to understand. "I could tell that... I mean, I thought... something about the way you talked about your sister's baby made me think you might want one."

"Yeah, you know, eventually."

He let out a slightly disgusted sigh. "My sisters do that, too. Why do some women think they need to apologize for wanting kids? People tend to assume they do anyway."

"Maybe that's why. We don't want people to think we wouldn't be practical about it."

"I suppose. Sometimes it's annoying that people tend to assume the opposite about guys."

My eyes asked for clarification because I couldn't think of the right words. He was hinting at a wonderful possibility.

He shrugged. "I'm just saying... there are a lot of dads and we don't all have to be talked into it."

Oh my goodness! Did Jon just tell me that he wanted to have a baby!? Did the man not have any sense of self-preservation? He was going to be changing diapers in my next fantasy. And it was going to start immediately.

He stopped suddenly and I worried that he saw something of my thoughts on my face. He looked a bit confused and said, "Didn't this used to be the cracker aisle?"

"I wouldn't know."

"Hmm..." He glanced over the shelves. "Well, I don't think we passed them so..." He started walking again. "Did you say your aunt *was* a therapist?"

"She passed away a few years ago, when I was in grad school."

"I'm sorry. How old were her kids?"

"They were both in high school when she died. I'm sure that was rough. Hey, this looks like mostly pet stuff. Should we skip this aisle or is there something you need?"

Jon shook his head. "No pets at my house. Let's move on."

"And you're still not going to tell me where that is?"

"Where what is?"

"Your house."

He looked amused. "Why do you want to know where I live?"

"It just seems fair because you know where I live."

"That's ridiculous."

"I think it's more ridiculous that you won't tell me."

"Have you considered that I might have a very good reason?"

"For being ridiculous?" I wouldn't have pressed if I thought he actually had a reason, but he was clearly having fun with me. He also teased me about the huge bag of frozen broccoli I put in my cart in the next aisle. Honestly, it was going to take me forever to eat it and I put it in my cart only because I was so distracted I hadn't picked anything up in a while. Meals that week were going to be interesting.

Mabel was working the register and Jon insisted I go first. She gave a slight gasp when she saw me. "Oh, hon," she said, "I heard George Baumgartner's dog died this week. Is he doing okay?"

"I think so. I'm sure his house feels empty."

She nodded sadly. "Mary Beth was also telling me about an empty house this week. Both of her girls are off at school now."

It didn't seem to matter that I didn't know Mary Beth. I just tried to look as though I was paying attention while Mabel told me which colleges the girls were attending and I got my random assortment of groceries onto the belt. Jon was helping me. That's why I wasn't really listening to Mabel. "Oh, that reminds me," she said abruptly, "I heard about you getting all cozy at the park with James' boy."

That got my full attention. "You mean Seth?"

"Yeah, that's his name."

Her expression said that this was a juicy topic and I did not want Jon to get the wrong idea about me and Seth. "He's only a friend," I said.

"You sure about that? Trudy said you two were awfully cute and-"

"I'm sure."

"Well, I'm kind of relieved to hear that. The boy has the attention span of a gnat."

I couldn't help laughing that she used the same expression as Caitlin. Was that a family thing or the way the whole town viewed Seth? I actually might feel a little bad for him if it was the latter.

Mabel said, "You do seem to be fitting right in anyway, hon. Making all kinds of new friends."

"Yes. I think you know this one." I nodded to Jon behind me.

"He helped you out all right last week I guess?"

"Of course." I looked at Jon watching us talk about him and had a sudden idea. "Jon was just telling me how to get to his house from here. What was the name of his street again?"

"Maple," she said. "That should be easy enough to remember."

"Yes, it should," I said, trying not to laugh at the expression on Jon's face. When my cart was refilled, I waited for Jon to finish. He was very quiet and only nodded as Mabel shared a few town details. It occurred to me that I might have made a tactical error. In my haste to clarify Seth as a friend I had thrown Jon under the same umbrella. And he heard me. What if he thought I put up the friend barrier on purpose?

On the other hand, that might make it less scary for me to suggest we see each other again. We could do something as friends and then... well, surely the whole marriage and family thing would be obvious to him soon enough.

We walked out together and I told him I was happy that I'd bumped into him. I believe I was able to make it sound like an accident. Then I said, "Do you want to maybe *plan* the next time we see each other?"

"Okay. What do you have in mind?"

"I enjoyed the pizza on Friday. Maybe we could meet there on purpose this Friday?"

"I know Caitlin has other plans so that sounds perfect."

We agreed on a time and we went to our respective cars. I surreptitiously watched him throw his bags into his backseat and drive off. He seemed perfectly relaxed and casual, not at all as anxious as I felt. I was worried that meant he was pleased our plans didn't sound like a date.

Chapter 17

Caitlin came into my office during a break the following morning. Her face was plastered with a huge grin. She said nothing as she sat in one of those little kid chairs. She kept grinning as she looked at me as though waiting for something to happen.

"What's up with you?" I asked.

Her smile didn't waver as she said, "You like Jon, don't you?"

"What makes you think that?"

"Mabel told me that you two were shopping together yesterday."

My instinct was to protect my feelings until I had some sense that Jon might return them. I tried to sound innocent. "We just happened to be in the store at the same time."

"Mabel said you guys seemed friendly and it occurred to me that maybe there was a reason you haven't put up a fuss when I suggest setting you two up."

"Do you want me to put up a fuss?"

"Just admit that you like him."

If Jon only wanted to be friends, it would be better for me to know that before I got my hopes up any higher. And if I could find that out through Caitlin instead of through an embarrassing disaster of a non-date… "I still don't know him that well, but you win. I admit I'd like to know him better."

"I only win if you use the word interested."

I sighed and gave up all attempts at being coy. "How do you feel about the words huge crush?"

The grin I didn't think could get any wider suddenly did. Caitlin stood and bounced on her heels. "This is awesome," she said. "And don't worry. I won't tell anyone. I'm just going to be silently rooting for you guys." She squealed slightly as she left my office and I doubted the silent part. I saw Ethan next and Caitlin was talking to Heather when I brought him back. Neither of the women said anything to make me think they'd been talking about me. I rushed back to my office anyway.

The day finished without my face turning red and when I got home, I finally got my newest zebra positioned on the wreath. I opened my front door to hang it up and was startled to find Riley standing at the base of my porch steps. "Hello," I said.

"Hi."

"Can I help you?"

"Um..." He moved up the steps and gestured to the wreath in my hands. "What are you doing with that?"

"I... That's a good question. I want to hang this on the front door here and I just realized I've never hung a wreath. I probably shouldn't put a nail in this door and I think it might just fall off then anyway." I held the wreath up to the door. There was a silver-toned door knocker. I tried to position the wreath so that it hung from the knocker but I could tell it would slip off before I even let go.

I turned back to Riley, who was watching me silently. "Any ideas?" I asked him.

He shrugged a bit. "Maybe you could use some string to tie it to the knocker?"

"Yeah, I could do that. I think that will work. Thanks."

He nodded at me and turned as if to leave.

"Riley?"

He turned back to me.

"Did you simply have some premonition that I was about to have a wreath-hanging crisis or was there another reason you came over?"

"I, um..." He smiled as he shook his head. "It's not important."

"Are you sure?"

"Do you need to get into the attic for any reason?"

"No."

"Then it's not important. Goodnight."

I still couldn't figure out what was going on with Riley Iverson. And I was beginning to wonder if it even had anything to do with me. I had mostly been ignoring Seth's texts. Some of them were funny but he didn't seem to have gotten the message about dialing back the flirting. That night he sent me a message that said: Time to take you up on that promise of a next time. Let's go for a drive.

I replied: It's a little late. I'm not going out tonight.

Seth: I could come over there.

Me: I don't think so.

Seth: Tomorrow for sure. I miss you too much to go another day.

Me: Okay. We can do something friendly.

Seth: I will sweep you off your feet and change your mind.

Me: I asked you to be serious.

Seth: I AM serious.

He was a little less charming from a distance. That and some time with Jon had pretty much cured me of any infatuation I had felt for Seth. If I refused to play along with his flirting on Thursday, I would likely find out if he had any intention of attempting a legitimate friendship. I tried to ask him during the day what he had planned for the evening and he replied with his typical bit about surprises being more romantic.

Caitlin and I didn't get a chance to talk much, but she stopped by occasionally to gloat about being a brilliant match-maker. Her gloating was premature and she hadn't arranged the date that probably wasn't a date yet. I still appreciated her optimism.

When I got home from work, I still didn't know if Seth was planning food or not. I had a quick snack that would leave room for more or tide me over if there wasn't. I changed into jeans and got a sweater handy. Then I sat down with a book while I waited to be surprised.

I thought I heard someone on my porch but there was no knock. I heard more footsteps a minute later and got up to look out a front window. It was Seth. I flipped on the outside light to see better what he was doing. He had a pumpkin in each arm and was gently setting them on a patch of newspaper he'd evidently spread on my porch. He grinned and waved at my window as soon as his hands were free. Then he ran down the steps towards his car. It was parked in front of my house with an open trunk.

He pulled two more pumpkins out and put them next to the others. I wondered if I should go outside or wait for him to ask. When he ran back to his car again I put on my sweater. He had a cardboard box in the next armload and he closed his trunk so I guessed it was the last trip. He deposited the box on my porch and pulled his phone out of his pocket. A few seconds later, I got a text that said: Your porch light knows I'm here. Why don't you?

I sighed and opened my front door.

"That wreath is new, isn't it?" he asked.

"Yes."

"Why does it have a horse?"

"It's a zebra."

"All right then. Are you ready to carve pumpkins?"

"Halloween is still two weeks away. Isn't it a little early?"

Seth smiled. The dimples were still cute. "These are practice pumpkins," he said. "Pick which two you want."

"Okay." I hadn't carved a pumpkin the previous October because they'd been smashed the two years before that. It did sound like fun. "Can I have this one?" I pointed to a taller pumpkin that was on the skinny side. The other three were fat and round and for some reason I liked the unusual one.

"Yes," Seth said, "and which one for your second?"

"The rest are pretty similar. It doesn't matter to me."

"Good choice." He pushed two of the round ones off to the side. "You sit there and I'll sit here and then our knees can bump."

I tried to give him a disapproving look. He successfully ignored it as he sat next to me and put the box between our pumpkins.

"I have lots of tools," he said. He handed me something with an orange handle and a jagged edge.

"Thanks." I began to study my pumpkin and asked, "What are you going to make?"

Seth had taken a tool identical to mine out of the box and was already sawing the top off his pumpkin. "Something very scary. I think. It will have big teeth."

I couldn't decide what to do with mine. I hoped an idea would come to me while I scooped it out. I began cutting the top. "I think I want something that's not a face but I don't know what."

"Not a face, huh?" Seth looked thoughtful. "How about a ghost?"

"Less scary."

"A smiling ghost?"

105

I considered that idea and couldn't figure out how I'd manage it. "I think that might be too complicated for me."

Seth gave me some puppy dog eyes and said, "You could carve a heart."

I rolled my eyes at him.

"I'm trying," he said.

I looked at my pumpkin intently. "Oh, I know."

"What?"

"Aren't you the one who likes surprises?"

"Awesome," he said with another grin.

We scooped fairly quietly. It was comfortable silence as we both had something drawing our attention. After a while, however, it felt less comfortable as I noticed that Seth's attention was not fully on his pumpkin. He was watching me out of the corner of his eye and the dimples popped out whenever he caught me glancing his way. I decided that we needed some conversation. "I bought that wreath from your sister, by the way."

His eyes moved quickly to the wreath and back. "I'm not surprised. She sells all kinds of crazy stuff. I mean, I like the wreath, but you gotta admit it's unusual."

"It is. That's why I like it."

"That's a good reason." He rummaged through his box of supplies and found a smaller carving tool. Then he turned his pumpkin around to pick a front before he poked the tool into it.

"How long have you lived in Hartford?" I asked.

"Um… twenty-four years."

"Is that how old you are?"

"Close. I'm twenty-seven."

I took a moment to focus on my pumpkin. The inside seemed clean enough. I picked up the same orange tool because I didn't think I'd need anything more precise.

Seth suddenly picked up a pumpkin seed and flung it into my front yard.

"What are you doing?" I asked.

"It's good luck."

"Who told you that?"

"Everyone knows it's good luck to toss one of the seeds when you're carving a pumpkin. It makes your picture better."

"I think you just made that up."

He shrugged. "It makes as much sense as any other superstition."

"I guess so." I flicked a seed into the yard as well and said, "Just in case." Then I concentrated on my carving while Seth worked on his. I looked over to check his progress. His pumpkin had round eyes with a bit of flesh in the bottoms shaped sort of like half moons. The mouth he was finishing was huge and had very pointy teeth. "Nice eyes," I commented.

"Thanks." He winked at me. "Yours are nice, too."

"I meant your pumpkin."

"I know. I didn't."

"Well, mine's done. What do you think?" I turned it to face him.

"A candle! That's great."

"I'm relieved you can tell what it is."

"It's obviously a candle. We'll put a candle inside the candle. Very clever." He pointed to the box. "I even brought candles."

I pulled out a small candle and put it inside my pumpkin, which I set next to my front door. Then I brought a second pumpkin to our work area. "This is fun, Seth. Thanks for bringing the pumpkins."

"You're welcome. How's this?" He turned his pumpkin towards me.

"Yikes!"

"Yikes it's bad or yikes it's adequately scary?"

"Scary."

"Good." He put his finished pumpkin next to mine and brought over the last one. "So, um, Angel... are you seeing any more of, um..." He gestured to George's house.

"Maybe, but not... George and I are only friends."

Seth nodded. He pulled the top off his pumpkin. "What's your next one going to be?"

I was still scooping seeds out of my pumpkin and I tossed one into the yard, which made him smile. "I think I'm going to do a face this time," I said. "I'm going with tradition and giving him triangle eyes and nose, but I haven't decided on the mouth."

"The mouth is the most important part. It tells you if the pumpkin is happy or scary or sad or... waiting to be kissed." His eyes were on my mouth in a way that made me nervous.

"My pumpkin is not waiting to be kissed," I said as I deliberately put a few more inches between me and Seth. He worked on his carving in silence. I tried to focus on mine but it bugged me that he seemed out of sorts. I was the one who had to keep reminding him not to joke around. I was beginning to worry that the evening would not end well.

He eventually jabbed his tool into the side of his pumpkin and said, "I'm done." He had carved an X for each eye and a mouth with an extreme frown.

"A little morbid," I said, "but it still looks good."

"Thanks." He appeared to relax as he took his finished pumpkin to join the others and returned to my side.

He peeked over my shoulder and said, "Went with a smile, huh?"

I had given my pumpkin a crooked smile with only two teeth and I was cutting out the last bit. Seth put a candle inside it for me and I picked up the lid. As I turned the top to see which way it would fit on the pumpkin, Seth put his hands on top of mine and he kept them there as the lid fell into place.

"Seth, don't…" I pulled my hands out from under his.

"Don't what? I don't understand what I'm doing wrong here. I thought we were having fun."

"We are but I told you…"

"You said we could be friends or we could pursue a serious relationship. I know which one I want." He tried to take my hand again.

I stood up while I tried to figure out what to say. I didn't know if this was some sort of line or if he'd convinced himself that was what he wanted.

He stood as well and faced me. "Angel, I can be serious. I am serious. How do I prove it to you?" His eyes had never been so intense and they were floating between my eyes and my lips. If it was a line, it was a good one.

My mouth was starting to move but I couldn't get my brain to put words into it. Finally I said, "I think we need to call it a night."

"Can I see you tomorrow?"

"I have plans and I don't think that's a good idea anyway."

"Why not?"

"If you're not satisfied being friends then we probably shouldn't see each other at all."

Seth blinked at me for a moment before he put on his usual winning smile. "I surprised you with this," he said. "You go on inside while I clean up the mess. I'll call you after you've had a few days to think about us."

He stressed the last word and began to busy himself with the cleanup. I wanted to tell him that I wasn't going to change my mind. But the truth was that he had surprised me. Equally true was the fact that I was a coward. If he was giving me the option to leave the awkward scene and talk about it over the phone later instead of face to face, then I was going to take that option. "Goodnight, Seth. Thanks for cleaning up."

He smiled and flicked one more seed into the yard as I went inside my house. I slowly and quietly slid the lock into place before I went into the kitchen to give my hands and forearms a good scrubbing. Pumpkin carving could be messy. It would likely be a lot messier with children. I wouldn't mind.

I tiptoed back to the front window and checked the porch. Seth was already gone. It was sweet that he brought everything over and cleaned it up, too. He was a lot of fun and I was disappointed that we weren't going to be hanging out anymore. But even though I didn't know him all that well, I felt sure that we wanted different things.

Chapter 18

I saw Parker at school Friday morning and something kind of strange happened. We had a normal, though brief, conversation about a fundraiser coming up at the school. It was as though we were suddenly rational colleagues. I guess time had helped.

Caitlin and I had lunch together and another woman from the office joined us for the first half. As soon as she left, Caitlin said, "I talked to Jon last night."

"And?" I prompted, assuming she brought him up for a reason.

"And nothing. He is so frustrating. I asked him if he was looking forward to seeing you tonight and I asked him if he thought it was going to lead to more dates and he was all like 'Back off, she's just a friend.' But I know him. Mr. Privacy wouldn't tell me anything even if you guys were picking out wedding invitations."

I paused to consider that for a moment. I liked rings. I hoped Jon wanted invitations with a simple pair of rings.

"So you're going to have to be the one to tell me if things get serious, okay?"

"We'll see if there's anything to tell."

Caitlin rolled her eyes. "You just better make me a bridesmaid. But you can say attendant because I don't want to be listed as a matron. That sounds so old."

"Counting some chickens, aren't you?"

"I'm just good at predicting who will be good together. And I have another idea. Do you know if George Baumgartner is going to get a new dog?"

I shook my head.

"If you see him and it comes up, you should suggest he try the shelter on Greengold Drive in the city. My cousin works there and I have a feeling those two would hit it off."

"I'll try to remember that, but I don't know if I really want to be your pawn."

"They do have dogs there," Caitlin said. "There's no harm in hoping he finds something else he likes."

"You're kind of hopeless, aren't you?"

"I am the best kind of hopeless. I once heard Jon say he likes the smell of cinnamon, if that helps at all."

"How would that help?"

She shrugged. "That's all the advice I have at the moment."

Caitlin gave me more drive-by advice later in the afternoon, telling me that Jon played baseball in high school and that he didn't like the nickname "grease monkey." She told me the latter as a first grader arrived for his session. The boy thought the term was hilarious and I had a feeling it might spark a recess game later in the day.

****

I was optimistic about seeing Jon again. We seemed to get along well and even if he wasn't interested in me the same way I was in him… that could change. We could be friends for a while and that would give us time to see all the things that we had in common. The chemistry would build over time until he finally couldn't resist kissing me, a lot. I didn't know how to make him find me attractive but I was also picturing "finally" as no more than a month so my fantasy didn't have to make sense.

Then we would have a long talk about the future and all the ways we envisioned it the same. There was no need to rush. Even with my slower plan, we could have that first baby by the time I was thirty-one. Ashley would probably have her second by then. That would be okay though. It would be okay.

I wore a touch of makeup for a change and a pink sweater. I knew Jon didn't need to be reminded that I was a girl. I still hoped that little feminine touches might nudge his brain into thinking we were on a date.

He was waiting at Pops for me outside the front door. My legs felt stiff as I approached him and I prayed that it didn't look as though I had forgotten how to walk.

"Hi, Angel. Did you walk from home?"

"Yeah. Is it weird that I had to think about that?"

"What do you mean?"

"I'm not used to the small town closeness. I was about to get in my car when it occurred to me that I'd only be driving... Would you say my house is even a quarter of a mile from here?"

Jon looked up at the sky for a moment. "I think that's about right."

"So I thought it seemed silly to drive except that it is a little cold and I thought walking might keep me warm and... It should not have been a difficult decision."

"I walked, too," he said. He turned quickly to open the restaurant door for me. I caught a glimpse of a smile. I wasn't sure if he was already enjoying himself or simply laughing at me. Either way, I was happy to hear that he had walked. What I didn't tell Jon was that my choice to leave my car was made by the idea that he might offer to walk home with me or give me a ride. The walk would take longer.

Pops had tables in the middle and booths along either side. Most of both were taken and a line of people were waiting for pick-up orders near the back. Jon ushered me to an empty booth on the left. Someone who might have been an employee dropped a pair of menus on the table as we sat but he didn't stick around or even greet us.

"It wasn't this busy last Friday," I said.

"It'll clear out a bit soon. The football team is home this week."

"You don't go to the games?"

"Only occasionally. I had a cousin on the team last year but he graduated so..." He finished with a shrug.

I nodded and opened my menu. I only pretended to read it while I looked at Jon. He had apparently gone home to change after work, unless he didn't work on Fridays, because he was wearing a dark green T-shirt with long sleeves. He looked great. I could not figure out why I was disappointed not to see the Hartford Garage logo. Somehow the plain clothes felt less intimate than when he let me see him in his work shirt, the one he wore in public something like forty hours a week. It made no sense. The laws of attraction are not laws at all. They are random and illogical ideas that sometimes cannot be explained by the people who come up with them.

We settled on a pizza and then Jon asked if I brought any broccoli to go with it. I might not have known what he meant

112

except that I'd thought of him every time I opened my freezer since Tuesday. And I thought of him when I stood next to it, too.

I smiled meekly and said, "How's the monkey liking your place?"

"I think he's lonely with no zebras around."

For a moment, I thought Jon might not be talking about a plastic monkey. I thought he might be saying that *he* was lonely, that he was looking for someone to share his house and his life. And then I recovered. I was imagining the man might want to marry me because he was mocking my zebras. Sometimes it was as though a twelve-year-old girl was taking over my love life and I wasn't even putting up a fight. I tried to focus on a simple conversation. "You said before that you gradually started working for your dad and you almost made it sound like you fell into the career. You did *want* to be a mechanic, right?"

"I did. When I said I gradually spent more time at the garage I meant my dad gradually let me spend more time there. I think at first I was not nearly as helpful as I thought I was."

"And you have two brothers but only one of them works with you. There's no hard feelings there I hope?"

Jon shook his head. "Chris never had any interest in cars so Dad never took it personally that he wanted to do something else. He's a CPA. It was almost weird with Emma though."

"How so?"

"She thought she wanted to be a mechanic and she worked at the garage a few years in high school. Then she had a hard time telling Dad that she had changed her mind. He took it well."

Someone – I think it was a different person than the one who dropped off our menus – swooped by to take our order. I wasn't sure how I was going to get food into my flopping stomach.

Jon said, "I, um… I heard Father John is retiring at the end of the year."

"He probably deserves the rest. Has he been at St. Christopher's long?"

"Eight or nine years I think. I know he's not the best homilist, but he was great in the teen program. I think he was responsible for a lot of us not walking away after Confirmation."

"What do you think he'd do if someone actually threw a hymnal at him?"

"Duck?" Jon said with a wry smile. "Really I think he'd be more worried about possible damage to the hymnal. The choir director is always freaking out about people not being careful with those things. If you sit close enough to the choir, I swear you can hear her sigh every time one gets dropped."

A man's voice answered before I could. "I'd take anything he says about Margaret with a grain of salt. There's a history there."

"Hey, Tommy," Jon said to the man who had appeared next to our table. Then he held out his hand to the small boy cowering behind his dad's leg. Ethan appeared mildly concerned to see me outside of school and his wide eyes didn't immediately take in the offered hand. Then he took it between both of his own and squeezed while intense concentration covered his face.

"Oh, no." Jon pretended he couldn't pull his hand free from the tight grip. He continued the fake tug-o-war while he addressed his brother. "You cooking tonight?"

Tommy nodded to the pizza box he was carrying. "Yes. You must be Miss Melling."

"I am," I said. "Angel when I'm not at school."

Tommy had the same dark hair and friendly eyes as his brother. His eyes were brown though instead of blue and slightly bloodshot. He had two or three days' worth of stubble on his face and the slightly worn-out appearance of someone with a newborn in the house. "Nice to meet you," he said. "Can't stay though. We need to get this home while it's hot."

At that point Ethan let go of Jon's hand and climbed onto the booth next to him. He whispered in Jon's ear for a moment.

"I'm sorry, buddy," Jon said. "You're gonna have to go with your dad."

Ethan pouted as he climbed down, then quickly recovered and sprinted to the door. Tommy waved as he chased after his little boy. I suddenly had several things I wanted to say or ask about and decided to begin with the obvious. "What history do you have with the choir director?"

Jon rubbed his hands together as though he was slightly embarrassed. "Well, I was in the choir for a while, only because my mom begged me. And then Margaret started bugging me to sign up as a cantor but I do *not* do solos." He shook his head to emphasize the point. "She kept asking and eventually it got uncomfortable that she wouldn't take no for an answer so I quit altogether."

114

"You must be pretty good."

"No, I'm really not. She's just kind of obsessed with the fact that all the cantors are women. She wants a balance."

I considered that for a moment, trying to remember if there had been any male cantors during my relatively short time at St. Christopher's.

"Speaking of balance," Jon said. "We seem to be talking about me a lot."

"The first time we met you gave the impression that Caitlin had told you enough about me."

He gave what might have been a guilty smile but it disappeared before I could appreciate it. "Does that mean you won't tell me anything else?" His tone sounded almost flirtatious. Or maybe that twelve-year-old was back.

"First tell me what you know."

"Not that much really. She told me where you grew up and that your parents are still there. I think she said your mom works at a grocery store."

"Is that all?"

I saw a hint of a smile before Jon nodded. There was something he wasn't telling me. I didn't ask. "Well," I said, "there's not much exciting to talk about with me. My dad is a mechanic, too, but he works on airplanes. My mom was a paralegal before she had kids. She quit when I was born and stayed home with me and Ashley. When we left home, she said she was just going to wait around to watch the grandkids. I mean, she did a lot of volunteer work so it's not like she was sitting around. But then when Ashley and I moved farther away after school, she started working part time as a cashier. She's trying to convince my dad to move now that Ashley's pregnant."

"My parents are excited about the grandkids, too. Ethan was supposed to stay with my mom the day Valerie was born but he begged to come to my house instead so Dad told me to take the day off. And yes, it is very mature that I'm bragging about how a three-year-old thinks I'm more fun than my mother." He seemed to roll his eyes at himself.

A steaming pizza was placed in front of us and I bowed my head briefly in silent prayer. I always thought my family was pretty great so I meant no disrespect to any of them when I added my

115

longing to join Jon's family. And talking about his family had given me a good opening for something I'd been wanting to say.

"Do you remember when you brought Ethan to school to see me?" I asked.

He nodded for me to keep talking as he pulled a slice of pizza onto his plate.

"The funny thing about that day is... um, the last time Heather was there she said her husband was going to bring Ethan."

"Yeah, that was the plan. But no one expected the little one to take so long. It was nearly midnight when she was born so I wasn't going to wait up for Tommy to drive back from the city and Ethan was already asleep anyway. It made sense for me to keep him longer."

Jon didn't understand what I was trying to say. I helped myself to a slice while I tried again. "I hadn't met Tommy yet so I... I mean I didn't even know his name so..."

"Oh, yeah. I was going to say that I was surprised that you just met Tommy tonight. I know he's taken Ethan to speech a few times, but I guess that was with the last teacher. Or, um, therapist."

My face felt a little warm. If I tried to explain a third time it would no longer be a casual remark. Maybe if I was quiet for a moment, he'd keep thinking about when he took Ethan to school and then something would click. I got through a few bites of pizza before Jon said, "The crowd has thinned now."

I glanced around the restaurant to see that he was right. I had been concentrating only on our booth so I hadn't noticed that the place had gotten much quieter. Several people were still scattered about and I felt an uneasy sensation when I realized that I knew one of those people. Seth was sitting by himself in a booth directly across from us. He was holding his phone and looking at me. I had heard and ignored a new text only a few moments ago. Was it from Seth? This was not a good time for his brand of spontaneity.

I stuffed a bit of pizza into my mouth and tried to chew naturally. Even with the sudden tension, the flavor was wonderful. My phone pinged again as Jon said, "Do you wear a costume when you pass out candy?"

"I have a costume, but I have no intention of wearing it."

"Why not?"

"It was Ashley's idea of a joke. We talked about wearing costumes a few years ago. I wasn't excited about it but told Ashley I'd wear one if she got some for us. Know what she got me?"

Jon shook his head and glanced at my bag sitting on the booth next to me. My phone had pinged two more times.

"It was wings and a halo," I said.

I think Jon would have gotten it sooner if he hadn't been distracted, but he looked confused for a moment before he smiled. "That's kind of funny."

"No, it isn't."

"Have you had people make fun of your name?"

"Not really. I... excuse me a second." I pulled the phone out to make sure it was really Seth and not some emergency. He could see I wasn't reading his texts so he kept resending the same one. It said: Make an excuse and come talk to me.

I could still feel him watching so I shook my head slightly before I silenced my phone and put it away. "Nothing important," I said to Jon.

He appeared relieved, probably more because I turned it off than because he had feared an emergency. "Is there a story to your name?" he asked.

"You mean because it's so weird?"

"No! I, um..."

"Relax. I'm kidding. I did get a bit of teasing when I was younger. I guess I was kind of a teacher's pet so people would make jokes about my angelic behavior in class. It was never mean-spirited though." I stopped to take a sip of my drink. "As far as I know, my parents just picked a name they liked. Does Jonathon have a story?"

"A very boring one. Tommy was named after our dad, Thomas actually. Chris was named after one of the grandfathers and I was named after the other one."

I had been purposefully not looking at Seth because I didn't want Jon to notice where my eyes were landing. I didn't know he had gotten up until he sat down next to me.

"Hey, guys," he said with a careless smile. I slid over a bit because I was too stunned to do anything else.

"Hello, Seth." Jon greeted him with a puzzled and wary nod.

117

Seth stretched his arm along the back of the booth behind me. He wasn't touching me but it felt possessive nonetheless. "I hope I'm not interrupting a date," he said.

"It's not a date." Jon was the one who answered and I felt myself deflate at his words.

Seth nodded as though that was the answer he expected. Then he winked at me and said, "What are you guys up to after the pizza?"

Jon shrugged. "We didn't plan anything else."

Seth looked at me. "So you'll be free soon?"

"No," I said. Seth's dimpled smile was suddenly not charming at all. Maybe Jon didn't think we were on a date and maybe he said that because he thought there was something going on between me and Seth. I wanted to blame Seth for the disappointment either way. "I'm not doing anything with you later even if I am free."

Seth kept smiling. "You're cute when you're upset with me. I thought we worked this out last night though."

He was trying to make it sound as though we were in a relationship. I looked helplessly at Jon, who was avoiding eye contact. He said, "Do you want me to go so you two can talk?"

"No," I said. "Seth and I can talk later."

Jon began to slide out of the booth. "You really shouldn't leave things unresolved."

That advice would have been awesome yesterday. Jon left some cash on the table and Seth casually thanked him. Then Seth pointed to the pizza and said, "Can I help you finish this?"

"No! What do you think you're doing?" I had tried to be polite and keep my composure in front of Jon, but now I wanted Seth to know that I was angry.

He appeared genuinely bewildered. "I thought you wanted help getting rid of him."

"Why would you think that?"

"Because you didn't know how to respond to my texts."

"I thought *not* responding made it pretty clear that I wanted you to get lost."

Seth had picked up a slice of pizza. He put it back on the pan before it touched his mouth and he grabbed a napkin. He didn't clean his fingers with it, just sort of fiddled with it. "I think I see," he said. His voice lacked the usual confidence. "When you said you were looking for a serious relationship, you meant with someone other than me."

I began to squirm against the realization that I might have underestimated Seth, that he might actually feel something for me, and my anger shrank. "It wouldn't work between us," I said. "I think we want different things."

He turned and put his arm along the back of the booth again. His fingers teasingly flicked hair away from the back of my neck. "Tell me what you want."

"What I want?" I repeated.

"Yeah. How do we make it work?"

I decided to open myself up to him. For once I wasn't worried about scaring a guy off with my wishes. "I'm looking for 'til death do us part. What I want is to get married. I want to start having babies right away, at least two of them. And I want a husband who won't just give me a zebra."

Seth's fingers pulled back a little. I don't think he did it knowingly, but it proved to me that his idea of serious and mine were not the same. He also addressed my least significant desire when he said, "What's wrong with zebras?"

"Nothing. I love zebras. But when guys give me zebras it feels as though they want to give me a present without having to think about it."

Seth whipped out a playful smile. "I gave you pumpkins."

"Do you go to church?"

"Uh... where did that come from?"

"You're the one who mentioned being serious. Do you believe in God?"

He shrugged. "I guess. I've never been a church person though."

"That's another reason we wouldn't work."

"Does your church have some sort of rule about-"

"It's not a rule. It's just... That would be a significant part of my life that you didn't share and that's not good for a relationship. There's just... There's not going to be an us."

Seth absently spun the pizza pan on the table and neither of us spoke while it turned and then slowly came to a stop.

"I can tell there's no convincing you," he said eventually. He smiled at me as he stood but with a sadness around his eyes that startled me. "The good news is that everyone will assume *I'm* the one who lost interest." He winked at me as he left.

I sat there staring at what was left of the pizza. I saw two guys on the same night again and yet I was no closer to that happily ever after I wanted. I didn't consider one of the guys a date and the other one hadn't considered me a date. Maybe. I couldn't tell if I had any hope at all with Jon. Things had ended awkwardly, but not badly. If I could figure out some way to see him again I might still be able to get Ashley into that pink bridesmaid dress I'd been picturing. And Caitlin would look nice in it, too. But even more than any fantasy I just really really liked Jon. I liked him so much those angry tears I'd fought off when he left were not only due to anger.

I left Pops and I left the uneasy feeling that people I didn't know were talking about me. I walked home alone.

Chapter 19

Saturday began very gray and the clouds got thicker and darker as the morning wore on. It was ideal weather for moping and I felt like moping. I stayed in my jammies and I ignored two calls from Ashley. I let myself think about how cute Jon looked with Ethan whispering in his ear. I wondered if there was some way I could sabotage my car so that it needed a mechanic without being obvious to that mechanic that I had done something.

I eventually had enough wallowing and I abandoned any thoughts of marching up and down Maple Street in favor of staking out the Market again. Jon was going to have to explicitly say he wasn't interested before I gave up. But there wasn't anything I could do about him at the moment. I called Ashley back and let her tell me about how the pregnancy seemed to have screwed up her taste buds.

The rain still hadn't arrived though. It was late afternoon and at least as dark as twilight and I had a sudden desire to watch the rain. I put a small pan on the stove to make some hot cocoa. When it was ready, I took a fuzzy orange blanket and a steaming mug to my front porch where two wooden chairs were waiting. I hadn't yet used them but the chairs looked as though Bill had cleaned them up just before I moved in. I claimed the one closer to the house so I could watch without getting wet and sipped my drink while I waited for the soggy recital.

A black car parked in front of my house and Riley got out of it. He made it halfway up my sidewalk before he noticed me on the porch. He visibly startled and stopped walking for a second. Then he resumed the trip at a slower pace.

He stopped before he climbed my steps. "Hello," he said and tried to smile. "I'm not here to evict you."

"Glad to hear it. What's your excuse this time?"

"Oh, I... um," Riley stammered. He was clearly flustered and I felt bad about calling him on the excuses.

"Hey, do you want to join me for some hot chocolate?"

He looked uncertain.

"Do you *like* hot chocolate?"

He nodded somewhat clumsily.

"Great," I said. "You can take this seat and I'll be right back."

I went into the house and grabbed a second mug. I topped mine off while I was at it and took them both back to the porch. Riley was sitting in the chair closer to the railing. He stood to take the hot mug from me. I nodded to the chair to encourage him to sit again. "So," I started, "I can't believe the rain has held off this long."

Riley nodded and said, "Yeah."

"Is the cocoa okay?"

"Yeah." After a pause, he added, "It's good."

He was definitely a man of few words. Somehow though, I got the feeling that wasn't because he was nervous about asking me out. I thought it was about time I figured out why he kept coming by. "It is nice to see you again," I said. I thought perhaps we'd begin with the excuse and go from there. "Did your dad send you?"

He smiled slightly and said, "Dad thought the power might be knocked out if it rains hard enough and I mean... you do have at least one flashlight, don't you?"

"I do."

"See?" He seemed to be implying that he knew it was only an excuse for him to head to my house.

"Do you know why he's making up excuses to send you over here?"

"He has ideas." He briefly moved his finger between us. "Are you sure you don't mind that I've been humoring him?"

"Humoring him?"

"Yeah." Riley took a drink from the mug and then looked as though a horrifying idea had just occurred to him. I think he was worried about offending me because he began to apologize profusely and nearly incoherently. "I'm sorry, I don't mean... it's not that I... you're, um... I mean, you're very pretty and all and... I didn't... it's not that he had a bad idea, I just... I sort of already, but you're... I didn't mean..."

"Riley, stop. It's okay."

122

He looked at me uncertainly.

"I understand. You already have your eye on someone else."

"Kinda." He looked into his mug and turned slightly red.

"Are you already dating or just hopeful?"

"Neither really."

"Do you want to tell me how you know her?"

"She, um… she works at Fred's."

"Have you asked her out?" I was being very nosy but it felt appropriate. He looked as though he wanted me to draw it out of him.

He shook his head.

"Are you going to?"

He shook his head faster.

"Do you guys talk much?"

"Not… I go to Fred's a lot. It's probably obvious to her but I keep telling myself she just thinks I don't like to cook and that is also true. I think she's just friendly to everyone. And she probably thinks I'm too old for her."

"What are you like thirtyish?"

"Thirty-one."

"And she's…"

"Twenty-four."

"That's not weird."

He shrugged. "I don't think so."

A freakishly impulsive idea struck me. "Do you think she's working tonight?"

He nodded.

"Let's go," I said as I stood and tossed my blanket aside.

Riley didn't move. He stared up at me with a very worried expression.

"Sometimes it's easier… I mean someone not involved might be able to tell if she's interested. It's worth a shot."

He still didn't move.

I looked at my watch. It wasn't quite five. "It's a little early for dinner but then she might be less busy. Come on." I took his empty mug and said, "I'm coming right back so don't run off on me."

I grabbed my purse from the house as I put the mugs in the sink. Riley was still sitting in the wooden chair on my porch as I locked the front door behind me. "I promise not to embarrass you.

If nothing else, we'll have a nice friendly dinner. And maybe someone will tell your dad that we were out together."

Riley gave an outright laugh at that and finally stood to follow me off the porch.

"Let's hurry. That rain is certainly going to start now that we're vulnerable. You take your car and follow me." I thought it'd be good if we didn't need to leave together, just in case. I didn't tell him that because he was nervous enough.

I parked outside the yellow brick restaurant and waited at the front door for Riley. I opened the door and he held it for me. We were greeted by the same dark-haired young woman who had made sundaes for me and Seth. I couldn't remember her name. She said, "Hi, Riley. Um, Riley's friend." She nodded at me and I couldn't be sure, but there seemed to be a weird emphasis when she said the word friend.

She led us to a booth near the back and then walked to a nearby table. She claimed two menus from that table and dropped them on ours as she said, "Pick something yummy and I'll be back."

I opened my menu. Riley did the same and studied it in a way that made me think he wasn't even looking at it. "Was that her?" I whispered.

He nodded very slightly.

"What's her name?"

He looked around us to make sure no one could hear and said, "Missy."

I nodded and focused on my menu. The room got much louder as the long-awaited rain began to pound on the roof. "What's good here?"

"I think everything is good… but I'm not picky."

"Okay."

Missy was back quickly and asked for our order. She wrote it down and turned to leave. Then she turned back to pick up our menus. She got halfway to the kitchen before she turned around again and dropped the menus on a table near us.

I leaned across the table slightly. "Is she normally a bit… absentminded?"

He shook his head seriously. "She's very good."

"I wasn't trying to… I thought she might seem bothered by you appearing to have a date."

"This was a bad idea."

"No, that's good. Maybe. Just relax. I'll figure out a way to clarify to her that we're just friends."

"This was a bad idea," he repeated.

"Relax, Riley." I tried to help by talking about something else. "So your dad sent you over to make sure I owned a flashlight?"

"He hinted you might get scared and need..." He stopped to show the annoyance with a sweep of his eyes. "I think he's worse than my mom."

"That is kind of funny. Did he send you to do the bushes before?"

Riley sighed. "You saw me?"

I nodded.

"I thought I could cut them real quick and you wouldn't even notice and he'd think I'd talked to you."

"Why were you humoring him anyway?"

"It seemed the safest way not to let on about, you know..."

I did know. And she was back at our table. "Here's a Coke," she smiled at Riley as she put it in front of him. "And your water." I did not get a smile. "You're the new speech teacher, right?"

"I am. Angel Melling."

The brief nod she gave as she left was unmistakably terse. I didn't mention it to Riley because it was possible that she had animosity towards me that had nothing to do with him, though I couldn't think of anything else I might have done.

Riley and I chatted for a minute. Mostly I asked questions and he gave one or two word answers while his eyes flicked around the restaurant. Was I that obvious when Jon was around or did it only seem obvious because I knew?

A chorus of gasps suddenly replaced most of the light in the large room. The drumming of rain on the roof was the only sound until a generator sparked dim backup lights and animated chatter. One person called out, "Well, this sucks," and another voice said, "If you still manage to burn my sandwich, I'll be very impressed." The second observation was met with laughter.

I looked at Riley. "It's a good thing I'm not at home where I might be scared, right?"

He smiled slowly. "But now you don't need a flashlight."

"Did you bring me one?"

He gave a sheepish shrug. "There was one in my car, but honestly I was about to turn around when I saw you on the porch."

I smiled at his admission. "Glad you didn't." Riley and I might form an actual friendship that made us both happy. Though he didn't say as much, I believed he was tentatively agreeing on the condition that we got through the dinner without me saying anything awkward to our waitress.

The conversation around us continued as tables seemed to have been joined by the lack of power. Missy appeared next to our table and said, "Hey, so obviously the food is on hold until we have something to cook with. Do you plan on hanging around?"

"Yeah, at least for a while," I told her. She was looking at Riley for an answer. He nodded with me.

"I guess this gives you less to do right now?"

"Yes, I can't bring out raw food," was what she said. Her tone asked why I wanted to know.

"Would you like to sit with us for a minute?" I suggested. "You're probably on your feet a lot." I moved over and she took the offered seat. Riley began fidgeting. I hoped I wasn't already breaking my promise not to embarrass him and that he only feared I might. I thought it best to keep the focus off him at first. "So Missy," I said, "how long have you worked here?"

"Three years or so."

"You've been in Hartford longer than that I presume."

"I grew up here."

"Well, you know I'm new so I'm just trying to get to know people… see if I can make some friends as I settle in."

"You don't seem to be having any trouble," she said.

There was a chilliness in her comment that suggested having trouble would be better. I suddenly understood. She saw me with Seth and had likely heard about Jon or George and now I was with Riley. She was thinking the same things I might think about a woman who came to town and immediately tried to date every man in sight. "Yes and no," I said. "I've been meeting some people but there's nothing happening with any of them." I meant to be up front without being quite so transparent about my utter disappointment in the dating arena. It did cause Missy to soften towards me.

"No luck, huh?"

I tipped my head in Riley's direction. "Present company excluded of course."

126

Missy's eyes darted questioningly between us and I clarified. "I mean the making friends part. I'm renting from Riley's dad and he's been very helpful, even trimmed my bushes. I thought a meal was reasonable payback."

"Oh, that is the most darling house. I've always wanted to see the inside."

"It's cute on the inside, too," I said. I don't think I imagined her relief that the evening out had been my idea and not Riley's. There might be a happy ending here if I had any clue how to play match-maker. Where was Caitlin when I needed her?

"So it wouldn't be awkward for me to ask about, um, someone else?" Missy said with another glance at Riley. He was so quiet we could almost forget he was there, except that his plainly thoughtful nature made us want to include him. And remembering his existence appeared to be enough for him.

I shook my head. "Go ahead."

"I just wondered if someone warned you about Seth or if you had to find out the hard way that he... um..."

"... has the attention span of a gnat?" I suggested.

She laughed. "Exactly."

"I was warned. I'm not sure that was entirely fair to him though."

"Oh, so you think maybe you're going to live happily ever after with him after all?" Missy looked amused and skeptical.

"No," I said, "but someone might."

"That's a nice thing to say," Riley said.

"I guess."

"Since you asked me about Seth," I said to Missy, "does that mean I can ask if you're seeing anyone?"

Missy looked at Riley and then looked at me and then looked at Riley again. She turned back to me and said, "I'm not. The thing about small towns is that if you don't meet someone in high school you might have to sit around waiting for someone new to move in."

"I don't know. You're less confined by age as you get a bit older so you might find someone who didn't go to school with you."

"You might," Missy said as she slipped out of the booth. "But you might get even older waiting around to see if he's missing your hints or ignoring them on purpose and I need to go check to see if there's anything I should be doing right now." She turned several shades of red before she made it to the kitchen.

I looked at Riley. He was calmly poking the ice in his drink with his straw. "And you thought this was going to be a bad idea."

He smiled bashfully and didn't say anything.

"Don't worry. I'll leave ahead of you to give you time to work your magic."

He rolled his eyes at me.

I didn't care. It felt good to be optimistic about a new relationship, even if it wasn't mine.

Chapter 20

I mustered more reverence in church that week than I had in a fairly long time. There was a brief pang when I considered that Jon was likely sitting on the opposite side and I was alone. I did not let my thoughts linger there. I thought about the fact that I had loving parents and a sister who would soon be thrilled to let me babysit. I liked Hartford and I liked working with the kids at the school. I stayed seated when others began to file out, closing my eyes to concentrate on the blessings in my life. I wanted to stop feeling restless and feel at peace with whatever life lay ahead of me. Instead I felt a tap on my shoulder.

"Can I interrupt?" Caitlin asked.

I moved over to give her room to sit next to me.

"I can't wait until tomorrow. You have to tell me right now what happened on Friday."

"What do you mean?" I glanced behind us to see if anyone was with her.

"Dan's waiting for me outside," she said, though that wasn't who my eyes had sought out. "So tell me what happened at Pops."

I bit the side of my lower lip. "What did Jon say?"

"Nothing," she hissed through an exasperated sigh. "People are saying that you ditched Jon for Seth Anderson in the middle of the date. Jon said, 'That's not what happened and it wasn't a date,' and he won't say anything else." Caitlin's gaze bore into mine as though daring me to admit that I had abandoned her brother. To me it felt as though the opposite had happened. But I would not accuse Jon.

"Seth showed up, uninvited," I said, "and he made it awkward enough that Jon left. I don't blame him but he wasn't the one I wanted to leave."

"Why didn't you tell Seth to go away?"

"I don't know. I mean, I did after Jon left. It just all seemed to happen so fast. And I kind of thought things were going well with Jon before the interference."

"What are you going to do now? Do you want me to give you his phone number?"

"I... don't think so."

"Why not?" She already had her phone in her hand.

"It just... no offense, but Jon seemed so adamant about you not being involved that I'd feel weird about calling and telling him that you gave me his number."

"That's actually a good point. What's your plan?" She leaned a bit closer.

"I'm hoping we'll keep bumping into each other and... well, eventually I'll figure out if he's interested."

Caitlin rolled her eyes. "That's not a plan," she said. "And it's going to take forever. I hope I can be as patient as you are."

I smiled at her as she left. I wanted to laugh at someone calling me patient in my husband hunting. Except that it wasn't funny. My plan was to patiently wait in a parking lot until I could follow my unsuspecting prey into the produce section. If I was talking about someone else, I'd say she had gone off the deep end. And I would not call her patient.

****

Jeff and Ashley were waiting for me after church. Ashley made soup for lunch and Jeff was trying to eat the steam as I arrived. "It's about time," he said. "Did you get a long-winded sermon today?"

"Not really. Isn't spiritual food more important anyway?"

Jeff looked at me for a moment. I wondered if maybe he didn't realize I was only teasing. Then he said, "I'd agree with you if anyone else was cooking."

"It does smell good," I conceded. I should have guessed he was only looking for a way to work in a compliment. Ashley smiled sweetly. At least she had the grace to look as though she knew how lucky she was.

I took a seat next to her while Jeff set the table and brought over the soup. I had already told Ashley about the disaster of Seth scaring Jon away so we let Jeff talk about work while we ate. The company he worked for made mobile games. I had never played their last game, something with a space theme, but what they were working on now sounded possibly fun. It was a card battle game and one of the artists had used a picture of Ashley to draw one of the princess cards. She was excited about that.

She was even more animated a few minutes later when she jumped up from the table. "Oh," she said, "I have to show you what I bought yesterday."

Jeff leaned across the table as soon as she was gone. "She wanted it to be a surprise, but I gave Mike your picture, too. Would you be upset about being in the game? It won't look exactly like you."

"No." I shook my head emphatically. "She'll be a powerful card though, right?"

He smiled at me and gave only a slight nod because Ashley had returned. She was holding a white plastic hanger with a yellow infant-sized sleeper hanging from it. "Isn't it cute?" she asked.

I took the hanger from her and felt the soft fabric between my fingers. "It's so small," I said. "Do babies really start this tiny?"

"I guess so. They were all that size."

"So you're stocking up on supplies already?"

"No." Ashley took the cute jammies back. "I only bought one. I wanted to get one by itself just so every time I put it on the baby I'll know it was the first thing I got. It's corny, I know. But I'll remember it was the first even when I get to pass it on to your baby. Someday." Her dreamy expression was all hope and optimism. I'd been looking forward to my niece or nephew all along. That was the first moment though that I felt truly happy for Ashley without the added twinge of jealousy. I asked her if I could come shopping with her when she was ready to fully stock up.

****

I got home to Hartford mid-afternoon. George was in his front yard trimming some bushes. We shared a pleasant wave. Things were going to be okay there.

I got comfortable with a book on my plush sofa, planning to be lazy the rest of the day. I hadn't been resting long when I heard my phone signal a new text. I was very relaxed and didn't want to get up. Curiosity won out before long and I dragged myself to the corner of the room where I pulled out my phone to check the message. Caitlin had sent: `Are you home?`

I replied: `Yes.  Why?`

Caitlin: `Jon is coming to see you.  Don't be mad.`

My heart lurched against my ribs as my eyes fell to the dingy shorts I was wearing. Jon wanted to see me? And Caitlin was giving me warning to clean up. How could I be upset about this? A sickening feeling came to the pit of my stomach as I made a guess.

I texted Caitlin: `What did you tell him?`

Caitlin: `I only hinted.`

Me: `What did you say?`

Caitlin: `Don't worry.  It'll be fine.`

I put the phone down. I didn't know how far away Jon's house was or how much head start he had. I didn't have time to argue with Caitlin. I darted to my bedroom and slipped back into the pink dress I had worn to church. In the bathroom, I pulled the clip out of the back of my hair and let it fall over my shoulders. I smoothed my hair with my hands and it didn't look terrible.

Then I returned to my living room and began to furrow a path in the carpet while I analyzed the situation. Caitlin had hinted something to her brother, something that almost certainly had to do with how much I liked him. And now he wanted to talk to me. That had to be a good sign, right? Unless… he had made that comment about it being bad to leave things unresolved. What if he was worried about having given me the wrong impression and wanted to set the record straight? It would be cruel to come all the way over here just to tell me he wasn't attracted to me. He wouldn't do that. This had to be a good development.

I nervously peeked out my front window and there was no one in sight. George must have finished his yard work. No sign of anyone walking up my sidewalk. I dashed back to the bathroom and brushed my teeth. There had been some onion in Ashley's soup and, well, just in case.

I paced for what felt like hours, occasionally stopping to push the front curtains aside. Ultimately, a real hour did tick by and still I had no visitor. I called Caitlin.

"Angel? Hi."

"What's going on?" I demanded.

"What do you mean?"

"Did you talk to Jon today? About me?"

"Wait… did he leave already?"

"I haven't seen him." I was taking frequent glances out the window as I talked. My front porch remained deserted. "That's why I'm calling you. What did you mean when you said he was coming over?"

"That's weird," Caitlin said. She seemed to be talking to herself, which kind of annoyed me.

"What's going on?" I asked again.

"Well, I called Jon this afternoon because… because I'm just not as patient as you are. I tried to be subtle, you know, just talking about family stuff. And then I slipped in a mention of how you were upset that Seth interrupted on Friday and asked him if he was going to ask you out again. He mumbled something about how it wasn't a date anyway and tried to ask if I sent Chris something for his birthday. I wouldn't let him change the subject and insisted that you wanted it to be a date and then he said – this is a direct quote – he said, 'Look, she made the boundaries clear, now let it go.' And then of course I had to tell him that he was an idiot."

I laughed, partly out of nerves and partly because I could picture that conversation so well.

"Jon was quiet for a minute after that and I could tell he wanted to ask what I meant and *didn't* want to ask at the same time. So I just told him that he should talk to you if he thought I was wrong. I offered your phone number and he said he didn't need my help and then he hung up."

"So he didn't say he was coming here?"

"No, but I called Mrs. Frost next. She lives across the street from Jon and I asked her to look out her window to see if he was going anywhere."

"You're kidding! You actually called his neighbor to spy on him!?"

Caitlin made an exasperated noise into the phone. "How do you think we keep such close tabs on each other around here? There's always someone looking out the window."

I let go of my curtains. "So he left his house and you just assumed he was headed here?"

"He was walking towards your street."

133

"Maybe he just went for a walk." I tried to keep the disappointment out of my voice.

"No. I texted him that he should call me after he visited you and his reply was rather rude so I know I guessed right. Still… it shouldn't have taken him more than ten minutes to get to your house. Oh! Maybe he stopped to get flowers or something first! He's probably not that bright, but I would be so impressed if he did."

I would definitely swoon if Jon showed up with a bouquet. Then I would make Caitlin a bridesmaid. "Well, it doesn't sound to me as though I'm going to have company," I said as nonchalantly as possible, "but I will let you know if he stops by."

"Okay. I have to go anyway because Dan wants to know what I'm making for dinner. If Jon doesn't show up we'll make a plan tomorrow."

I hung up feeling curious about what scheme Caitlin was going to invent next. She was proving herself a bit more devious than I anticipated. But I still thought running into Jon at the Market was my best plan. My face was fully flushed from all the pacing and false hopes. I stepped outside. It was bright yet very cool. I was so warm that the brisk air felt like a pleasant contrast.

My feet walked down my sidewalk and turned to the right. Even though my dress had long sleeves, I'd be cold if I stayed outside too long. I could make it to Maple Street and back though. Even if Jon wasn't headed to my house, Hartford wasn't that big.

My short walk had a potential hiccup. I'd have to walk past Walt and Carol's house. I approached slowly, ready to turn around early if I detected anyone on the porch. There was a large tree blocking the front of their house. An older woman's voice drifted through the orange leaves with the words, "A girl? How nice."

Before I could change course she said, much louder, "Jon said they had a girl."

Jon? Was she talking about the same Jon I couldn't get out of my head or did I simply assume that because I couldn't get him out of my head. I continued slowly past the tree, trying to pretend that I was simply out for a stroll while casting furtive glances through the leaves in the hope that I could see what was happening on that porch before anyone saw me.

I nearly succeeded. Carol called out to me as I was processing the scene. Jonathon Thorpe was sitting between the older couple, strategically hemmed in against the front of the house. All three of them were holding playing cards and Jon's eyes lifted to the sidewalk at Carol's greeting. He didn't look delighted or let down to see me. The only emotion his scrunched expression conveyed was confusion. This was likely due to the fact that Carol had called me the wrong name.

"Gloria!" she called again. "Get yourself up here and say hello."

I nodded as I moved up their sidewalk. They were nice enough people and with Jon in the mix, I wouldn't mind stopping for a chat. But just before I reached the porch I had an even better idea. "Good afternoon," I said. "Carol... Walt... how are you tonight?"

"Pleased to see you, dear," Carol said.

"You'll catch a chill with no jacket, Gloria." Walt was sitting on the porch swing and he shifted the blanket on his lap as though offering me a warm place next to him.

"My name is Angel actually." I said it as loudly as I could. Walt's face showed no comprehension.

"Angel?" Carol shrugged. "How did we get that wrong?" She turned to her husband and yelled, "Her name is Angel."

He nodded unconcernedly and then patted the open space on the swing.

"I'm sorry to interrupt," I said, "but I was hoping to borrow Jon to help me get my car started."

I noticed that Jon put his cards down at my words.

"Of course, hon," Carol said. "He'll be delighted. Everyone in Hartford is always helping everyone else." She began to shoo him off the porch.

Walt waved to us both and I heard Carol yelling something about car trouble as I turned my back. Jon was following me and I was suddenly nervous. I'd been focusing on how much I wanted to talk to him and hadn't actually figured out what I wanted to say. And I was even more worried about what he might say. Had he been trying to find me as Caitlin believed or simply taking the agenda-free walk I was pretending to take? And maybe he was happy playing cards with my neighbors. I thought we should first make sure he was okay with friendly attention from me. "I hope you don't mind that I pulled you away from the cards."

He shook his head. "I hadn't intended to visit them in the first place. I mean, they're nice but it's like you don't even know you've been sucked in until you realize you can't get away."

"How long were you on the porch?"

"Forever," he said as he slipped his phone out of his pocket to check the time. "Okay, more like an hour." He gave me a wry look that completely counteracted the autumn chilliness. His presence affected me more than temperature. Everything around me faded into the background as I was so keenly aware of Jon being near me. He might have been wearing his church clothes as well because I could see a white collar under his navy jacket. The distance to my house grew shorter as the silence grew longer. I was beginning to feel self-conscious about having made up an excuse for Jon's company.

"So what's wrong with your car?" he asked.

He didn't know. Apparently, I was only getting a head start on the awkwardness. I caught the side of my lower lip between my teeth and said, "Nothing. As far as I know anyway."

Jon looked as though he swallowed a smile before he glanced at me. "You lied to get me off the porch?"

"I only asked if you could help me start the car. I didn't say it would be difficult." I tried to offer an innocent shrug. "It seemed like a good idea at the time."

"I'm not complaining. It's just... Do you think they can see your car from their porch?"

Caitlin's voice echoed in my head about there always being someone looking out a window. "Maybe we could take a look just for show."

"Do you have the keys?" His eyes looked me up and down and seemed to take in my empty hands and lack of pockets... and something else, something that made him look away quickly.

He was nervous! A little bit of flirting might just put us on the right path at last. First things first though. "I'll have to run inside for the keys."

He nodded and I cut through my front yard at a faster walk. I grabbed the keys and came back to where he was standing at the front of my car. He looked great waiting for me. I could almost picture a church around him and a priest waiting, too.

There was a loud click as I popped the hood. Jon lifted it and used the metal stick that he probably knew the name for to hold it in place. I came around and stood next to him, close enough that our shoulders were almost touching.

He placed his hands on the front of the car and leaned forward slightly. I copied the stance with the little finger of my right hand overlapping his left. I had a good feeling, but I wanted to be sure so I was trying to be obvious. Jon did not move his hand.

"Why don't you tell me something about what we're looking at?" I suggested.

"You want a lesson?"

I shrugged. "You can pretend to be explaining the problem to me."

"Is that why you're under the hood with me?" He was looking down at our hands. He wanted to be sure, too.

"I'll start by telling you everything I already know about cars," I said and picked up my hand to point. "That's the battery."

He let out a soft chuckle that stopped abruptly when I put my hand back down covering a bit more of his.

"It's new actually. This very cute mechanic I know put it in for me." If I flirted any harder I was going to sprain something.

I didn't know if it was nerves or just his personality that made him keep trying to hide his smiles, but when he mashed his lips together it was even more attractive than a full grin. I decided to go ahead and sprain something, though it didn't feel like a conscious decision. I leaned across our overlapping fingers and kissed him. It was the boldest move I'd ever made and I pressed my mouth only gently to his. He treated my lips to a response that said he was okay with me being bold. He tasted like cinnamon and wedding cake, though I might have imagined the latter.

I had to step back to catch my breath and my car's engine gradually reentered the scene. Jon also stepped back and he slowly and deliberately lowered the hood. It snapped back into place before he turned to face me. I was sure he was happy, but his eyebrows were also slightly knitted. He put his hand up to rub the back of his neck and said, "You turned me down?"

"I know. I tried to explain that."

He looked at me expectantly.

"Heather told me her husband was going to bring Ethan and I didn't know her husband so when you showed up..."

"You thought I was married to Heather," he finished for me.

"Yes," I said. "Married."

"Oh!" His expression darkened a bit. "You didn't think..."

"No, no. I didn't think you were suggesting anything inappropriate. I just thought you were, you know, being neighborly. I wasn't interested in neighborly."

Jon flashed a smile and then seemed to wipe it away with his hand. "If I tried again then?"

I nodded towards my house. "I still have leftover pizza if you're hungry and want to pick up where we left off on Friday."

"Okay. But can I ask a favor first?"

"What is it?"

"Well, if we go inside right now, it's going to look like I couldn't fix this." He patted my car's hood.

I had forgotten we were putting on a show and after the ad libs I hoped no one was watching. I played along anyway and climbed inside to start the car. It hummed nicely for a few moments before I shut it off. I closed the door behind me and said, "Look at that. You're a genius."

He laughed and said, "Thank you."

We walked up to my porch together. He reached into his pocket before I could grab the door handle. "Hang on," he said. "I got a little something for you."

I watched as he took a small rubbery-looking monkey and stuck it into my wreath next to the zebra. They looked good together.

"You like monkeys now?" I asked.

"It's not me, it's the zebras. I'm telling you monkeys are all they can talk about when they're alone."

"You're telling me my zebras talk to each other when they're alone?"

"Look at him," Jon said as he pointed to the one on the wreath. "He's clearly chomping at the bit to go inside and tell the others about the monkey who's just moved in."

"Now I know you're making things up," I said as I opened the door. "Because that zebra is clearly a girl."

Jon shrugged as though he was giving up trying to convince me of anything and he followed me into my house. "Did you stop by to see your sister while you were in the city today?"

"I did."

"Did it make you wish you were still living with them?"

"Of course. I always miss being the constant third wheel." I smiled at him and we shared a look that seemed to say he was thinking the same thing, that I could bring him with me soon to even the number. I did not suggest it out loud though. I got out the leftover pizza and worked to warm it up. Jon didn't like his pizza cold either and it was wonderful to find such an important thing in common.

We shared a few laughs, one of them over that hideous zebra statue I still hadn't gotten around to hiding. As he reached for a second slice, Jon took a deep breath and said, "Okay, I think we need to talk about something serious now."

Serious? It was probably a little early to talk about engagement rings but maybe he wanted assurance that Seth was no longer in the picture.

When I asked what he wanted to talk about though, he said, "Caitlin."

"Caitlin?" I repeated.

"Yeah. I know you think she's great and all, but my sister is the nosiest person in the world. I think we need to agree not to tell her anything."

"Why not?"

He gave me only half a smirk as he said, "Because it will drive her nuts."

"You want me to help you be mean to your sister?"

"It isn't mean to force her to mind her own business. And she gets so worked up when she thinks she doesn't know something. Trust me. Being quiet around her is more fun."

Jon's tone was light as he talked about giving his sister a hard time. But we were still talking about something serious. By asking me not to tell her anything, he was saying that there was something to tell. And there was. We sat there talking about anything and everything long after the pizza was gone.

He kissed me again before he left, inside the door because I had neighbors. When I reluctantly opened it for him to leave, I caught another glimpse of my latest zebra. Jill was wrong about it being my last one. I continued to collect zebras for a long time. It was, however, the last time I bought a zebra without thinking I was bringing it home to talk about monkeys. Jon made sure of that.

~~The End~~

Thank you for reading Collecting Zebras. Reviews are always appreciated.

Andrew's Key (January 2014)

Talk around Hartford is that the old Hilson house is haunted. Its new owner, Rebecca Hilson, doesn't believe that. She's more concerned with the decades of junk that has accumulated and for which she is now responsible. She doesn't know what to do with any of it or even how to approach sorting through it all.

Her new neighbor, Andrew Lately, is happy to offer some words of wisdom and the help of his grandson, Charlie, to get her started. Charlie makes it clear right away that he is interested in more than helping Rebecca move boxes. She doesn't know if she can return those feelings. In fact, recent events have made her question her ability to feel much of anything.

Will Charlie's patience pay off or will it take a real ghost to help Rebecca understand the nature of love?

Jealousy & Yams (April 2014)

Luke Foster has been accused of being too nice for his own good. He enjoys being helpful though and never thought it was a problem until he met Summer. Now he believes she feels indebted to him and it isn't gratitude he wants from her.

Summer Slough feels guilty for using Luke. She also feels an attraction to him that she doesn't know how to handle. It's beginning to look as though her mistakes and inexperience will keep them apart.

Lucky for both of them, Hartford's annual Yam Fest is right around the corner. The community event has a way of bringing people together… maybe even Summer and Luke.

The Christmas Project (coming November 2014)

Also by Amanda Hamm

Meet Cute: 5 Romantic Short Stories (2013)
5 stories… 5 couples… 1 cute collection…

THE SLOW LANE – Slow traffic on the way home from work is never any fun. Or is it? When the good-looking guy in another car starts flirting with Mia, she ends up enjoying the commute and the surprise it brings.

MY BROTHER THE MATCH-MAKER – Tabby's brother likes to play match-maker. She insists she doesn't want his help. Will Tabby have to admit she likes the guy her brother picked for her or will she finally see her good friend as something more?

WAITING FOR THE BUS - Wes isn't waiting for the bus. He always knows exactly what time it arrives. He knows what time she arrives to wait for it. Can he figure out the mystery woman? And will he have a chance to capture her attention as well as she has captured his?

NOW IS GOOD – Emily and Zane get two chances to meet two years apart. What happens when only one of them remembers the first time?

PIZZA HEAVEN – Pizza Heaven has mouthwatering food and a fun atmosphere. It's a dream job for most of the college students who work there. Kara in particular doesn't want to leave and she's attached to something besides the pizza. The problem? She doesn't have the courage to tell him.

The 4th Floor Lounge (2012)
Where does an extreme introvert draw the line between being
lonely and being left alone? One quirky college student is looking
for the answer in the 4th floor lounge.

Her goals are simple: make one or two good friends and avoid
talking to everyone else. Achieving those goals will not be easy for
this gorgeous yet socially awkward heroine. She's constantly
approached by guys who are not interested in friendship. And when
she finally forms some solid bonds it's her own romantic feelings
that get in the way.

www.ingramcontent.com/pod-product-compliance
Lightning Source LLC
Chambersburg PA
CBHW030533130626
46552CB00006B/2231